GARDEN
OF FANTASY

Karen Rose Smith

A KISMET™ Romance

METEOR PUBLISHING CORPORATION
Bensalem, Pennsylvania

To Liana and Anne Marie, my critique partners. Thank you.

KAREN ROSE SMITH

Karen Rose Smith is a former English teacher. When back surgery interrupted her lifestyle, writing romances became a creative and emotional outlet. Karen resides in Pennsylvania with her husband of twenty-one years and their nineteen-year-old son. She's always believed dreams are within her grasp if she does everything she can to reach them. Her family, peaceful surroundings, sunshine, and kittens bring her joy.

ONE

Beth Terrell's yellow compact car sputtered and gave a grunt after she turned off the ignition. She bet the snazzy Corvette parked behind her never made such noises. When she climbed out of her car, her dress wrapped around her legs and her tousled brown curls flew off her forehead. The stiff August wind sent black clouds skittering across the sky.

She hoped to heaven the rain would hold off until this meeting was over. If it poured, her car might not start and she'd be stranded at this isolated spot in the hills of Lancaster, Pennsylvania. Maybe she'd have to hitch a ride with Osgood in his limousine. She chuckled. That was one way to get to know him.

Another gust of wind buffeted her and she realized there wasn't even a construction trailer on the plot of land in front of her, nor a temporary structure, either. Just a purple and yellow canopy and a six-by-eight-foot sign proclaiming OSGOOD ENTERPRISES.

Forgetting about the weather, she hurried toward the canopy, her purse under her arm, her briefcase swaying as she walked. She was already a few minutes late and she wanted to impress Tobias Osgood, not give him doubts about her punctuality. She needed this project to put her in the ranks of the "known" landscape architects. She was still trying to prove her worth to the professional community. Starting over had been difficult, but not as difficult as moving to Lancaster, away from her family.

Gingerly, she walked toward the gathering, smiling as the tall grass and dandelions tickled her calves. The stretch limousine and uptown cars along the shoulder of the road were no surprise. Osgood was known to travel in style. He was also known to be an eccentric. She reminded herself to be prepared for anything.

As she approached the canopy and her hair whipped into her mouth, she found she wasn't prepared. Silver serving dishes perched on an immaculate white linen tablecloth that covered a long table. A butler in a tuxedo poured champagne while two maids stood behind the serving dishes. Beth recognized Osgood's long-jowled face from the society and business pages. She almost burst out laughing at his attire. A wild green, yellow, and red shirt hung loose over shorts of the same pattern. And was he actually wearing flipflops?

Luckily, he wasn't watching as she turned her head to hide a broad grin. She looked into a pair of piercing green eyes. Impetuously, she asked in a low voice, "Is this for real?"

The tall man standing next to her met her smile with a charming one of his own, though his tone was wry. "We're dressed for the occasion, but *he's* not. Only the orchestra's missing."

He cocked his head, appraising her with interest. His eyes roved from her wildly tossed curly brown hair down the basic white dress adorned with a sterling squash blossom necklace to her spike-heeled white pumps. "I'm Nash Winchester. Are you one of my competitors?"

So *this* was Nash Winchester, landscape architect extraordinaire. He was nationally known for his amusement parks and golf courses. Did she stand a chance against him? Sure she did.

"Beth Terrell," she answered. "How many of us are here?" She shifted her eyes away from him with difficulty, but his dark hair—thick and vibrantly healthy—lingered in her mind's eye. It was tapered over his ears and hung fashionably longer in the back, gently wavy.

After a quick glance at the two men standing to one side, and realizing she was the only woman present, she took a second longer look at Nash, telling herself any woman would. Nash Winchester. It sounded like a name from a western. In the charcoal suit with its gray and almost-unnoticeable-lavender pinstripe, he belonged in an office, not out on the range. But with those slim hips and long legs, in jeans he'd look as sexy as any Marlboro man.

Nash's gaze caught hers and she felt like a butterfly pinned to a board. Did he know about the fiasco in Virginia? Even though it had been over three years, did he recognize her face from the newspapers?

His expression gave nothing away as he answered her question. "Osgood invited four of us."

The awning overhead rippled as the wind picked up velocity. Tobias Osgood clapped his hands and made himself heard over the conversations. "I'd planned to speak to you about business first, but I'm afraid we have to eat and run. August weather's as unpredictable as I am." He chuckled at his humor.

As Beth looked toward Nash, his eyes twinkled and he shook his head. For some absurd reason, she wondered what might make him laugh out loud and if his laugh would be as rich and deep as his speaking voice. She caught herself. Uh-uh. He was her competitor. Besides, she wasn't sure the liberal dose of trust she'd been born with had been revitalized yet. Time did heal, but sometimes the process seemed to take forever.

Osgood continued. "As you enjoy dinner, I'd like to get to know each of you. Since we might suddenly have to take flight, I expect to see all of you again tomorrow night at my house." He nodded toward his butler. "Hanson will give out directions. Bring your bathing attire and we'll have a poolside picnic while I explain the details of my project. For now, enjoy the boeuf bourguignon and chicken cordon bleu."

Beth rolled her eyes to the peak of the tent. "Just what I need, a gourmet meal and a swim. I want to get to work on the preliminary layout for the resort."

She was puzzled by Nash's expression. Where there had been amusement was now something serious. Sadness?

It was gone when he responded, "No one can figure out how Osgood's mind works. I've been trying for years."

"Have you worked with him before?"

"No. I tried once a few years ago, but he chose another architect. That's not going to happen again." His eyes issued a challenge. "Not if I can help it."

"And what if you can't?" she asked impudently, deciding tact would never be her strong suit.

He seemed taken aback. "It won't be from lack of trying. I don't give up anything easily, Ms. Terrell."

Beth bet he could count on one hand the projects he'd wanted that had slipped through his fingers. He'd created and executed more landscape designs than she could count. Professional magazines always did pictorials of his latest creations. Golf courses had to get boring, but all of his had drama and character that made them unique. And the amusement parks! They were mechanically perfect to the last detail, down to the drainage systems, but fanciful enough to capture an adult's imagination as well as a child's.

Beth looked closely at his expressive face. It had plenty of character, with small lines to prove it. Had his personal or professional life put them there? Before she could ask another question to discover how he'd lost Osgood's last project, lightning zigzagged across the evening sky. The thunder smacked like an airplane breaking the sound barrier and she jumped.

Unruffled, Nash said, "Here it comes. So much for supper."

Rain splattered; leaves and twigs whirled in the wind as the poles anchoring the canopy began to sway. Men in white coats and slacks ran from the delivery truck by the side of the road toward the serving dishes as the flames warming them blew sideways.

Nash laughed, a clear, deep rumble as fascinating as the thunder. "I guess Osgood's caterers are going to save the food." As one corner of the shelter twisted to the right, he suggested, "We'd better save ourselves. Are you going to make a run to your car?"

For whatever good it was going to do her. "I have no choice," she mumbled as she followed Nash to the edge of the awning and peered into the steady downpour.

He waved to the swaying grass before them. "Ladies first."

She didn't need gallantry; she needed a raincoat!

Her briefcase would have to do. After three steps, she knew the heels had to go if she didn't want to break her neck in the long grass, or at the least, fall flat on her face. Because she scooped up her shoes and tried to hold them and her purse in one hand, Nash sprinted a good two yards ahead. She attempted to balance the briefcase over her head, but the maneuver did no good since the wind was blowing the rain in all directions.

Beth reached her car, biting her tongue in exasperation as she threw her briefcase and shoes on the passenger seat and slid behind the wheel. She turned the ignition once. Sput. Sput. Cough. She turned the ignition twice. Grr . . . wheeze. The third try told her this car hated wet weather as much as she hated liver. She had to do something fast before everyone left. With an unladylike oath she put on her shoes.

Grabbing her briefcase and purse, she hurried to the Corvette and rapped on the window. Nash wound it down. Feeling like an idiot, she said, ''My car won't start. Could you give me a ride into town?''

He seemed to hesitate a moment, a moment that seemed like a trillion years with the rain striking the back of her neck.

With a glance at her high heels wobbling on the roadside gravel, he got out, took her arm so she was steady, and escorted her to the passenger side. He opened the door, then dashed back to the driver's side, climbed in, slammed the door on the rain, and rolled up his window.

It had been a long time since she'd met a gentleman. Something inside her smiled, but she mentally slapped her hand and chastised herself to watch out. Courtly manners didn't mean a gentleman lived on the inside. She'd thought John was a gentleman. She'd thought he was a friend. But friends don't use each other, and a gentleman wouldn't benefit from ruining the reputation of a woman he supposedly cared about.

As she closed the door of the navy Corvette and her briefcase slipped to the floor, the smell of genuine leather wound about her. She looked at Nash and their eyes ran over each other at the same time. A laugh began in her chest. When a drop of rain trickled from Nash's hair down his nose, her merriment sprang free.

After a self-deprecating grimace, he laughed with her and swiped at his face with the back of his hand. He had a nice laugh. Warm, generous, as rich as his voice.

Beth shook her head, letting loose drops run down her face. "Is this really in the line of duty? I feel more like one of the Three Stooges than a professional."

Nash couldn't seem to pull his eyes from hers. "It makes you wonder what else he has up his sleeve."

Although the words were commonplace and casual, some kind of friction hummed between them. She lowered her eyes, trying to cut the circuit, and searched in her purse for a tissue. When she found it and dabbed at her face, she noticed Nash's gaze had dropped to her breasts. The silk jersey was discreet when dry. Wet . . . He must be able to see her nipples.

Beth's hands grew clammy and she shifted in the bucket seat, hoping the material would stop pressing against her. She shivered as the tissue disintegrated in her hand. "I'm sorry to inconvenience you." She rubbed at the tan leather. "I hope this doesn't mark permanently."

Nash's hand stopped hers from moving nervously over the seat. "Don't worry about it. I'm as wet as you are."

His fingers were hot around hers and she wondered why when everything around them seemed to be wet. She shivered again.

Dropping his hand quickly, he said, "You're cold. Let me get the heat on." He switched on the ignition, flipped the heater to high, reached to the floor of the back seat, and pulled up a grey flannel jogging jacket. "Here, wipe off with this and put it around your shoulders."

"But you—"

He unbuttoned his suit coat and shrugged out of it. His shoulders looked broader in the pale gray cotton, and the shirt almost popped a button across his chest as he flipped the jacket to the backseat. "That took the brunt of it. The shirt's dry."

Beth couldn't help noticing how his pleated damp slacks draped his thighs. Thighs that looked as hard and muscled as the rest of him. *Stop looking, Beth. He's a competitor. And you're not ready to trust a man yet. Especially a man who wants the same project.*

She cleared her throat. "If you could just drop me at the first gas station with a phone, I can call my secretary."

"You *are* going home."

Uh-oh. Authoritarian note. Beth sighed with relief. Knock him off the list. Her mouth formed a fake, sweet smile. "I don't have much choice, do I? Unless I want to drip all over my office and catch pneumonia." She slipped his flannel jacket around her shoulders, pulling it across her breasts, and was aware of a trace of cologne and something more male. It had the effect of a smooth glass of sherry. She reminded herself where she was and with whom she was riding.

"Sorry," he mumbled as he pushed the wet thatch of hair from his forehead. "I didn't mean to insult your intelligence, but I've known both men and women who put work before their health."

Authoritarian or caring? Hmm.

"I'll be glad to take you home," he continued. "Where do you live?"

"At Ashley and Orange. It's across town."

"That's on my way. I live in a development off the Fruitville Pike."

That settled it. She would be stupid not to take him up on his offer.

As Nash drove, he glanced at her, once, twice, a

dozen times? Beth felt more and more jittery with each glance, as if she were being sucked into quicksand or something more dangerous. Since the situation with John, she'd tried not to be alone with men unless it was professionally necessary. She didn't think she was paranoid. She just believed in self-preservation and learning to trust her instincts again. In time, she could. But this wasn't the time.

So she chattered. About the weather forecast, about the corn crop, about living in Lancaster and the Amish way of life—riding in buggies, living in houses with no running water, living off the land.

When she stopped for a breath, Nash asked, "Have you lived here long?"

An innocuous enough question. Maybe he didn't know about Virginia and Senator John Winston. "It'll be three years next month."

"What brought you here?"

"My roommate from college was raised on a farm in the area. I used to come home with her and fell in love with the countryside—the rolling hills, green pastures, its pure wholesomeness. I decided it would be a nice place to live. The rural area is quiet, the city busy; all of it is expanding in leaps and bounds and full of opportunity. I figured at twenty-eight I should start planting roots." She was fascinated by his hands on the wheel. Long fingers, large palms, a smattering of fine brown hair on the back.

"No family roots?"

Beth wondered if this was a casual conversation or a fishing expedition. His question was accompanied by a quick but probing look that seemed to carry her to a deserted island where only the two of them existed. A woman could enjoy fishing with a man like this.

She touched her wet dress so she knew exactly where she was. Being a romantic could get a girl into a lot of trouble. "I have family. But I'm an only child and my parents tend to be overprotective. I needed a place of my own, a life of my own. They're only three hours away." Far enough to miss them, but far enough to remove herself from Leesburg and gossip.

Enough about her. It was time to put the emphasis on Nash. "What about you?" she asked lightly. "You've been all over the country. Why Lancaster?" He smiled and her heart galloped. It was such a nice smile.

"My roots are here. My sister and I grew up in Lancaster. When my career began to get . . . all-encompassing, I missed Shannon and her family and decided to make a few changes. Settling here was one of them."

Beth was sure there was much more to the story than that. Someone like Nash didn't make a major life change on a whim. Maybe he'd experienced an early midlife crisis. She'd heard he was thirty-six. She'd also heard he was divorced. Not that it was her business.

"Leaving a life behind is difficult," she mused, thinking about her own situation.

"Not when it involves mistakes and painful memories."

"I guess it depends on the person. Running away versus finding a new life." She kept the defensive note in her voice to a minimum, or so she thought, until another probing look pinned her to her seat.

"Maybe there's no difference," Nash suggested.

She didn't comment and only broke the silence to give Nash directions to her house. When he made a turn without her telling him to, she tried to relieve the awkwardness she was feeling. "You know where you're going."

He nodded. "Usually. I don't like to get sidetracked."

"A narrow focus and one direction. You sound like

my mother. She's always told me to keep my eyes on the endpoint.''

''You don't?''

''Sometimes the unexpected is more exciting. I don't want to lose out on life by being too pragmatic. My father calls me creative.''

Nash grinned. ''And your mother?''

Beth sighed. ''She says I have my head in the clouds too often.''

''What do you think?''

''I think I achieve my goals with a combination of creativity and hard work.''

''Then we're not so different.''

Nash slowed down the Corvette to follow the house numbers. He parked at the curb and through streaks of rain peeked at the Victorian monstrosity looming over them like something out of a gothic novel. ''Is that yours?''

''I wish! I rent the downstairs.'' She tried to see its immensity, its gables and bay windows through his eyes. ''You can't see its beauty today. All the gingerbread trim, its character.'' The house had a personality. It was secure and protective and when she was inside, she felt as if she had a safe hand on her shoulder. How could she explain that?

Nash's brows arched. ''I'll bet the repair bills are hefty. But I also bet the nooks and crannies have more charm than any house on the market today.''

A glow warmed her heart. He was practical yet had an aesthetic eye. Heavens! Now she was acting as if she knew the man. He was a stranger with good and bad qualities like everyone else. Never mind the sexy bod and staggering smile. She consciously called up emotions of disillusionment and betrayal. She needed something to armor herself against Nash Winchester.

Beth quickly slid forward and grabbed her briefcase.

When Nash turned toward her, gracious upbringing led her to ask, "Would you like to come in for a cup of coffee?"

Green fire flickered in his eyes for an instant as his gaze seemed to swallow her. There was male appreciation, male desire . . . male fantasy? Had she just issued a come-on? "I mean, I'm grateful for the ride and you could dry off . . ." She trailed off, wondering if she was making matters worse.

A slow, lazy smile twitched up the corners of his mouth. "I'll take a rain check. Okay?"

She was grateful for the pun and kept her sigh of relief to herself. "Sure."

As her hand unlatched the car door, he said, "Tomorrow evening has to be an improvement. Don't forget your swimsuit."

His tone suggested he'd like to see her in it. But she skipped that to protest. "Osgood isn't serious!"

"Who knows? He might give the project to the one who can swim the most laps." She must have looked shocked because he admitted, "Maybe that's going too far. But not by much. You'll probably have the edge as it is. He's partial to women, particularly young, pretty ones."

Nash sounded matter-of-fact but there was an underlying thread. "That sounds like a warning."

"It is."

"Are you warning me against Osgood or warning me not to use feminine wiles to win him over?"

He appraised her steadily. "Osgood has a certain charm, especially for women with their heads in the clouds."

She bristled. "If you're talking about his money . . ."

Nash shrugged. "It has a persuasive quality."

She found the most formal tone she could muster. "Mr. Winchester, I want the contract, not Osgood's money." She straightened in the seat, sliding toward the door. "Furthermore, my professional life depends on my capabilities—not my sex."

With a twinge of guilt she remembered that John's capital had set her up in Lancaster. But that was different. It was his fault she'd lost her job and her reputation. He owed her. Besides, she was paying him back. Next month she'd send the final payment.

Thunder grumbled and Beth prepared herself to spring out of the car and run. Politely, she said, "Thanks for the ride," then opened the door and sprinted for the house.

As she reached her porch, she could picture Nash's last enigmatic smile, and as she inserted her key in the lock, she realized she was still wearing his jacket.

An hour later, pretending to buck his nephew off his back, Nash used his shoulder muscles to give the four-year-old the ride of his life.

Davie giggled and held on tighter as his brother Jason yelled, "Ride 'em, cowboy!"

Roger, the oldest and used to bossing his brothers, called, "Hold on with your knees. Wave your hands in the air."

Nash's sister rescued him a few minutes later. "Okay, boys. Give your uncle a break. He's not Superhorse."

"Aw, Mom."

"Not yet."

"You're not tired, are you, Uncle Nash?"

Nash laughed at the simultaneous dismay, gently shook Davie from his back, and sat on the living-room carpet with his arms propped in back of him to hold him up. Bending his knees, he grinned at his sister. "Superhorse?"

Shannon's long straight mahogany-brown hair slipped

over her shoulder. "Come to think of it, you don't look like a horse. But you look thirsty. Come into the kitchen and get a glass of lemonade."

Shannon's sons were waiting expectantly, as if hoping Nash would turn down their mother's offer and keep playing. He didn't want to disappoint them. "Let me talk to your mom for a little while, then we can play a game of Yahtzee before I tuck you in."

Appeased for the moment and at Roger's direction, the boys nodded, put a video in the VCR, and clicked it on. Nash shoved himself up and followed Shannon to the kitchen. She took a Tupperware pitcher from the refrigerator and poured lemonade into the glass Nash pulled from the cupboard.

Nash rearranged the knit shirt sticking to his shoulders, glad he kept clothes at his sister's. He stared at Shannon. She was pretty, although *she* thought she was fifteen pounds overweight. He didn't think so and neither did her husband, Wayne. But Shannon was always trying to perfect herself, to become more, to become better. He respected her for that, but he wished she could simply relax and enjoy who she was.

"What's up, Nash?" was her unexpected question as she handed him his drink and caught him off guard.

"I don't know what you're talking about."

She emitted an unladylike snort. "This is Shannon. The sister who knows you better than you want to believe. You're distracted and I want to know what's cooking. Problems at work?"

"No. Everything's smooth." At Shannon's leveling glare, he figured she wouldn't give up. He might as well pacify her. "I . . . met someone today."

Her eyes widened. "A woman?"

With a "sometimes I wish you weren't my sister look" he answered, "No. A zebra with orange-and-green stripes."

She ignored his defensiveness and pressed. "And?"

"And nothing. She got to me, that's all. She wasn't your usual cool, suit-dressing, sophisticated business-woman. Just forget it. I probably read her all wrong. Must have been the weather."

Shannon planted her hands on her hips and looked him square in the eyes. "We have something to talk about, brother, and it has nothing to do with the weather."

CENTRE OF GRAVITY

TWO

Shannon was as protective of him as he was of her. She'd probably noticed his recent restlessness, his dissatisfaction with life in general. And as always, she was going to tell him what she thought.

Nash pulled out the chrome-backed kitchen chair with his bare foot, sat down, crossed his arms behind his neck, and rocked back. "I can see it coming. Lecture five thousand ninety-nine."

Shannon narrowed her eyes. "This is nothing to kid about."

Shannon cared; she worried. Too much. "A good sense of humor makes life easier," he philosophized, hoping to take the course of the conversation in another direction. Preferably away from him.

"Your life isn't easy. It's lonely."

"Not with you and Wayne and those three leprechauns in there," he protested.

"You know we love you, but you need more than us. Do you ever add up how many hours a week you spend at your house, *not* figuring in sleeping time?"

His chair hit the floor as he unfolded his arms. "I suppose you have it counted down to the minute."

"You're exasperating!"

"And your antennae are working overtime."

Shannon rolled her eyes. Changing her approach, she touched her brother's arm gently as she sat down beside him. "It's been six years since Christy drowned, four since you and Monica were divorced. Don't you think it's time you let someone in?"

"Christy would've been nine years old last month," he said quietly.

"She's probably sitting in heaven on a cloud, wondering why her daddy's sad." Shannon radiated compassion, not pity because she knew he wouldn't accept it.

"I'm not sad."

"You're not happy." Her voice said she was sure.

"I'm somewhere in between like most people."

"Talk to me, Nash."

He leaned forward on his forearms and closed his eyes for a moment. Shannon and Wayne had been as supportive as any two people could be without being effusive . . . without prying. He owed them. "When I'm alone in the house, sometimes I think I hear Christy's footsteps or her laughter."

"You do. In your heart."

After a long pause, he admitted, "I think about Monica sometimes."

"Do you still love her?"

He rubbed his chin pensively, not having given the idea much thought lately. "No. She focused all her energy into selling real estate so she could forget. I didn't want to forget."

The memories were bittersweet. "I wanted to remember everything about Christy—the sound of her voice, the way she jumped up and down when she was excited, how she tried to touch the sky with her toes when I pushed her on the swing. I stopped talking about her because the pain in Monica's eyes was too hard to face.''

Shannon surveyed his face, searching. ''You've never been open to discussing your marriage before. Did you divorce because of what happened to Christy?''

There were so many reasons. The situation had been too complicated to merit a simple answer. ''Eventually I tried to face life Monica's way by forgetting the past and going on. But I saw a future with more children. Monica wouldn't consider it.''

''So what's going on with you now?''

He was grateful Shannon didn't push for more details. He'd shared more about his marriage in the last five minutes than he had in the last four years. ''Now I'm restless. The emptiness is getting to me. I thought spending more time with you and the kids would help.''

''But it hasn't.''

''Not enough. And when I met that woman today, something about her . . . jolted me.'' She'd had a friendliness that was out of place in the business world or even in today's society with everyone so self-absorbed and afraid to get involved. She didn't wear a polite mask, but a sincere expression of what she'd thought of Osgood and the surroundings. And Nash had responded to it—without thinking, without calculating, without examining.

Shannon shook her head, trying to understand. ''I don't get it. You're around attractive women. The woman you took to the play last month could've been a model instead of a dentist.''

''This lady's different. Something on the inside lights her up.'' In the car she'd surprised him by being less friendly. And nervous. It was strange. He hadn't changed his attitude. He'd been a perfect gentleman, never mind the racy thoughts when he caught a view of her dress plastered to her breasts. He wasn't exactly a stranger. Sure, she didn't know him, but she knew *of* him. He'd seen it in her eyes. So why the nervousness? It must have been the embarrassment over her wet clothes.

Shannon broke into his thoughts. "You could ask her out."

If circumstances were different. "There's a problem. I have an ulterior motive for wanting to get to know her. I always try to learn what makes my rivals tick. That way I can usually predict the style of their designs. In combination with their past achievements, I know what I'm up against. Beth Terrell hasn't done anything major to this point, so I have to learn her style from her."

Shannon's green eyes were puzzled. "You try to figure out what they're going to do so you can do the same?"

"Hell, no! I try to figure out their pattern, to see if it fits the client. If it doesn't, I cross them off my list of competitors. If it does, then I plan better, bigger, more exotic." The other two architects, Rosenthal and Adams, usually stuck to what had worked in the past, the known, the traditional. Unless Osgood's taste had shifted to the ordinary, they were not a serious threat.

His sister shrugged. "So, for business reasons you have to get to know this . . . Beth. Why don't you combine business with pleasure?"

Nash shook his head vehemently. "I don't do that, Shan. That's asking for trouble. This project's worth a lot of time and money. Too much to risk it for a fling."

"You think a fling is going to erase the emptiness? Ha! You're not the fling type."

Sisters. Shannon thought she knew him backward and forward. "I'm not a 'type.' I'm just trying to figure out how to handle this without getting sucked in."

"Would getting involved be so terrible?"

"Shan, I don't know if I'm ready. I don't want to make my life or business any more complicated than it is."

As if sensing Nash wouldn't share more in the silence that followed, Shannon confessed, "My life's going to get more complicated." At his raised brows, she added, "I'm going back to work."

"Do you want to?"

She moved restlessly in her chair. "Wayne's going to open his own security-system business instead of working for someone else's firm. He's tired of the trips out of town and so am I. So we need extra money until he gets the business going."

"I could help."

Her sparkling green eyes sent him a thank you. "Wayne won't let you."

"His damn pride." Nash picked up his lemonade.

Shannon clucked her tongue and defended her husband. "*Male* pride. You'd be the same and you know it. He wants to take care of his own family."

Nash thought about it for a moment. "I do understand. But you don't want to go back yet."

She avoided his gaze. "I didn't say that. Paralegal work has always fascinated me."

"But?"

She smoothed her dirndl skirt over her knees. "I feel guilty."

Nash was about to take a sip of lemonade, but at her words he put down the glass. "I don't understand."

"It's Davie. I don't like putting him in day care. I always said I'd stay home until all of them were in school."

"It's only for a year, honey." Nash tapped her wrist. "He'll be in kindergarten next year."

"That'll mean a half day with a baby-sitter. I know I'm a mother hen, but I want to be here for my kids."

Nash knew why she felt so strongly. "The way Mom tried to be, the way Dad never was."

Shannon raised her eyes to the heavens. "Thank goodness Wayne is a terrific father and husband. I can depend on him as Mom could never depend on Dad. I know he'll always be here for me."

"You two are lucky." Nash took a long swallow of his drink.

"You could be, too," Shannon said agreeably.

He wondered.

His beach towel hooked over his shoulder, Nash squinted against the sun as he walked toward the red-wood deck surrounding Osgood's strawberry-shaped pool. Swimming in backyard pools was difficult . . . would probably always be difficult. If only the gate had been locked, if only Monica had watched their daughter more closely, if only he hadn't planned another out-of-town park.

He closed his eyes against the sun and the memories, hurried his pace, and found himself at the edge of the deep end. When his gaze found Beth Terrell, a rush of hot desire zipped down his spine. Auburn lights wove through her curls, blinking at him in the sun when she tilted her head. Her turquoise one-piece bathing suit was modestly cut at the breasts and crisscrossed her back, but as she talked and gestured to Rosenthal, a colleague Nash had beaten out of more than one project, he saw high-cut legs that made his stomach clench.

Get a grip on yourself, Winchester. She might be a bathing beauty, but she wants Osgood's business as much as you do.

Nash needed to study the projects Beth had designed. In his travels, he'd made friends all over the country. From asking around, he'd learned Beth had worked for a firm in Virginia before she moved here. Jack Reynolds, a friend who lived in D.C., was going to send him information about her work, and pictures, too, if he could get them. Then Nash would know what he was up against.

Dropping his towel on the deck, Nash stepped up to the diving board. After a quick bounce and clean cut through the air, he swam a few laps, and without making a conscious decision, bobbed up next to Beth. He slid his hands down his face to wipe off the water and shifted his weight to his left knee to take pressure off the right. The old basketball injury had been bothering him lately.

Beside him, Beth laughed. "You look almost the same as the last time I saw you."

She tilted up her head, allowing a few curls to straggle over her earlobe. Yep, he'd remembered correctly. She was natural, fresh, friendly. And flushed. From the August heat, he guessed. Her cheeks grew even rosier when his gaze slid from her head to her toes and he said, "You don't."

She wrinkled her nose and two enchanting little lines creased it. "I don't usually work in a swimsuit. But I'll do anything to snare a prospective client."

Was she joking or serious? He felt his jaw muscles tense. "Anything?"

She smiled. "Within legal limits."

"What about ethical ones?"

She looked as if she wanted to sock him. "You do have a one-track mind. I believe businesses are run on honest principles and most people play by the rules."

Damn! He was too sensually aware of the curls falling over her brow, her suit clinging to her breasts, her creamy shoulders. "It's happened before. A woman with your appeal could get this resort on merits *other* than professional ones."

She didn't answer but moved past him. "I'd better

get dressed. The picnic's supposed to begin at seven. I can't say it's been a pleasure talking to you.''

Nash wanted to keep her from leaving, to talk to her just a little longer and prove himself wrong, but he berated himself for being foolish. *Business. Keep your mind on business.* The reminder didn't keep his eyes from following the graceful sway of Beth's body as she climbed the steps.

Beth slipped the pink, gauzy blouse over her head, careful not to smear her lipstick, then stepped into the matching skirt. Picking up the silver medallion belt strung on white leather, she tied it around her waist, then slid her feet into white sandals.

As she stuffed the wet suit into her duffel bag, she pictured Nash's muscular shoulders, his hair-covered chest, then his face. It was craggy and lean—he wasn't model-handsome. But he *was* sexy. The sensual lower lip, the jut of a tapered jaw, the long well-proportioned nose, the swath of hair over his forehead that she suspected knew its place and stayed there when it was dry. The man had the power to make her forget her name. She couldn't believe she'd tried to flirt with him. And look where it had gotten her. Into an argument.

Keep your distance, Beth. Her experience with John had shaped her responses to men, colored her instincts until she was no longer sure of her judgment.

She left her bag on the coral vanity. Osgood had told her to make this, one of five lavish bathrooms, her own for the evening. Heeding Nash's warning, she'd watched Osgood carefully. He'd been friendly but respectful.

When she'd finished dressing, she decided to take a look around the grounds, not knowing how long the picnic and meeting would last. Slipping out a door, Beth found herself in a side garden. Gigantic hanging planters overflowed with bridal wreath and fuschia. Boxwoods trimmed in the shape of a wagon wheel framed a bronze sundial.

A deep voice flowed over her shoulder. "Kipperling from Texas designed this. What do you think?"

Nash. She'd recognize that voice in a crowd of fifty. What was he doing here? Following her? Her pulse quickened and she concentrated on a broad stripe of late-afternoon sun falling across the grass.

She was determined to keep her manner businesslike after their encounter in the pool. "It's traditional. Well executed but not extraordinary."

He eyed her solemnly, then grinned, took her hand, and pulled her to the rear of the garden. "Then tell me what you think of this, Beth."

He made her name sound feminine, musical, compelling. Curious, she followed him without protesting. Around a segment of hedge, she saw a colorful orange-and-yellow profusion of African daisies interwoven with ferns, marble statues of cherubs, and red roses.

"Ooh!" she breathed as the invigorating hues titillated her senses. Then she remembered. This was business. "It's a rare combination, but it works well. The roses add a wonderful smell, the marble a shiny, cool contrast."

Nash looked like he was suppressing a smile at her change of demeanor. "It's inspired," he agreed. He checked his watch. "But we don't have time to appreciate it now."

She realized Nash was still holding her hand. The contact gave her a comfortable feeling. For about two more seconds. Then she felt self-conscious for enjoying the rough and smooth places of his hand, its warmth, its protection. Wiggling her fingers, she pulled back, all too aware they were alone.

A playful smile quirked up the corners of his mouth

as he released her. "I can't decide if I like the swimsuit better, or that. It's the same color as cotton candy."

She felt her cheeks grow warm. "Shorts seemed too casual." She glanced down Nash's white knit shirt and pale-yellow slacks. That was an imprudent move. Her heart fluttered. "We'd better get back to the picnic," she said brusquely.

Nash walked silently beside her as they passed through two more gardens, both different from the others. Beth concentrated on their design, rather than on Nash. One thing she knew about Osgood already. He liked variety.

Nash's arm brushed her elbow. "I didn't mean to embarrass you. Now or in the pool. It's just that I'm uh, used to seeing working women dress more conventionally."

He looked uncomfortable, as if he'd stepped on her toes. She hated to make anyone uneasy. "Tailored is boring. I don't know who decided women had to dress like men to be good in business. And you didn't embarrass me. Working solo has its disadvantages, one of them being a scarcity of compliments. I guess I've forgotten how to accept one."

He thrust his hands deep in his pockets. "You haven't always worked alone?"

A question that could lead to an unpleasant discussion. She'd learned to be honest but to give as little detail as possible. That way no one made connections. "When I left college, I worked for a large firm that covered a broad scope of services from contracting to interior decorating. We handled jobs from start to finish."

"The problem with that is, enthusiasm dims. One project starts looking like another." His voice carried disdain for the cookie-cutter approach.

"Exactly. I was ready for a change." That was no

lie. Circumstances had merely pushed her out sooner than she'd anticipated.

Cognizant of Nash at her side, she recognized the mild scent of chlorine. Was it sticking to his skin or hers? She glanced at him. His complexion was more tanned than hers. Would he have a swimsuit line around his hips? She grew warm imagining him naked. Since when did she indulge in . . . voyeurism?

Beth was thankful when they arrived poolside. The picnic had moved to the adjoining flagstone patio. Osgood himself, wearing a chef's hat and apron, was flipping hamburgers while two maids scurried around a table laden with food.

"Grab a plate," their host invited. "Help yourselves. The baked beans will get cold. Don't forget the chili. It's my grandmother's recipe."

Nash stood aside to let Beth step in front of him. With a quick look at him, she realized he did it without thinking and would have done the same for any woman. She felt respected and that made her feel good. During John's divorce trial, her self-respect had reached a low point. She'd called herself every color of stupid for being naive. Although her parents had bolstered her and *she* knew she'd done nothing wrong, criticism from outside sources had taken its toll. Would Nash believe her side of the story? Or would he, too, draw mistaken conclusions based on circumstantial evidence?

Why was she even wondering? After tonight they'd go their separate ways.

In addition to filling her plate with a little of this and a little of that from the crystal dishes on the table, Beth chose a bowl of chili rather than a burger. Two white wrought-iron chairs were positioned closer together, four others scattered along the pool's border. Nash sat down in the chair beside her.

Devoting her attention to the food, Beth kept quiet

and took a spoonful of the cheddar-topped chili. As soon as she raised it to her lips, Nash warned, "You'd better be careful. It's—"

As the chili hit her mouth, her tongue tasted fire. Her throat felt the singeing heat next, and when she swallowed, she knew she'd feel the spices the whole way to her stomach.

Nash grabbed his cup of punch. "Here, drink this fast to wash it down."

She grasped the cup and downed the liquid as fast as she could. Her eyes were watering and she feared her face was lobster-red. She felt like an idiot!

Nash leaned close to her ear, his warm breath fanning her cheek. "Hold on, I'll get you another glass."

While she opened her mouth to let air help cool it, she searched for a Kleenex in her purse, covertly glancing at the other two men who were still heaping their plates and talking to Osgood. Thank God they hadn't noticed.

Nash was back with water this time. She gulped it down and leaned into the back of the chair, finally feeling less uncomfortable. "My gosh! Did his grandmother formulate that recipe, then decide it was too potent for her generation so she had to hand it down?"

Nash chuckled. "I think Osgood embellished it. It's hotter than the last time I tried it."

"I didn't see you gasping for water! Do you have a steel throat and stomach?"

His eyebrows hiked up, giving him a roguish look. "I only take small forkfuls at a time. You scooped up half the dish."

"I did not . . ." She saw he was teasing her, so she smiled. "Thanks for the help. You saved me from causing a scene."

"You don't like being the center of attention?"

Beth's inner alarm went off. Nash wasn't just being

friendly. He was probing to know more about her. She felt pleased, yet scared at the same time. Nash learning about her, her learning about him, was an exciting idea. But not a relevant one.

Her manner was casual. "No, thank you. Being in the center ring of a three-ring circus doesn't turn me on."

"What does?"

You. Thank God she hadn't said it out loud.

But it must have glowed like a neon sign in her eyes. Nash reached forward and brushed a telltale tear from her cheek with his forefinger. For a moment she was stunned . . . stunned that such a gentle touch could cause a squall of turmoil in her chest. It unnerved her, so much so that she jerked away. His eyes held hers with such intensity her hands trembled. She reached for the dish that had tilted on her lap and lowered her chin. The charged moment passed. *Remember, after tonight you won't see him again.*

Nash moved back, fished his plate from the flagstone, and picked up his hamburger. With a wicked grin, he asked, "Wanna bite?"

She suppressed a smile. "No thanks. I'll concentrate on the deviled eggs."

As Beth ate, she tried not to be distracted by Nash and his long, lean presence. Relief passed over her when Osgood stood and demanded the group's attention.

Untying his apron, he flicked it over one of the tables, took a pair of thick horn-rimmed glasses out of his shirt pocket and settled them on his nose. "Now we get to the nitty-gritty of why you're here. Last evening, we were blown from the site of my next resort. I wanted you to get the feel of the surroundings, but I suppose you can do that on your own." He picked a pack of papers off the cocktail table and handed a packet to each architect.

"These are the building specifications and the parameters of the acreage. You have free rein. I've kept the cost down on the structures because I feel the grounds are more important. Do your magic. I'm not interested in the lowest bids. I want inspiration. Let your imaginations run wild. I've chosen the four of you because I'm impressed with the work you've already accomplished."

Whipping off his glasses, he poked them at the group for emphasis. "I want to make one thing perfectly clear. Your presentation is due on September fifteenth at one P.M. in my office. Your oral presentation and explanation of your concepts will be as important as your sketches and boards. You will draw lots to decide who will go first, second, third, etc."

With a professorlike look at all of them, he said, "I know you'll do your best." He returned his glasses to his pocket. "That about sums it up. Any information you need is in the packet I've given you. Now, let's enjoy dessert and iced coffee."

Beth turned to Nash as naturally as she would have turned to a friend. "That's it? All this hoopla for a five-minute speech?"

"He's one of a kind." Nash patted the papers on his thigh. "But he's right. Everything we need will be here. These get-togethers are to look over the people he's considering. And believe me, he's had his eye on you all evening."

She wasn't oblivious to what went on around her. "You're wrong. He's had his eye on you as much as me."

Nash's expression said that few people challenged his observations. "You could be mistaken."

One of his looks could level someone. She ignored it. "Nope. Osgood's subtle but sharp. Look at him. He's pretending to be interested in choosing a dessert, but his eyes are on Rosenthal."

Nash looked taken aback by her perception and inclined his head slightly. "What do you think he's learning?"

"I don't know. But I'm going to join him at the dessert table and go on the offensive." She stood and walked toward Osgood, feeling Nash's eyes on her back.

Osgood saw her coming and held out a dish. "Carrot cake?"

"Thank you, but I'll pass. I do have a question, though. I'd like to tour your factory and grounds as soon as it's convenient. Is that possible?"

His bushy gray brows arched over his eyes. "Of course. Anytime. Just come by my office and I'll show you around myself."

"Nine o'clock tomorrow morning?"

He looked at her speculatively. "You don't let grass grow under your feet, do you?"

"I try not to." She extended her hand. "I must be going. But thank you for the swim and picnic."

"A heavy date?" He winked.

"A heavy workload." She winked back.

Osgood laughed out loud. "I like your style. Straightforward. I'll see you tomorrow morning."

As Beth went into the house to retrieve her duffel bag, she remembered Nash's jacket in her car. Hopefully his car wouldn't be locked and she could throw it inside. She didn't like to be impolite, but leaving now was better than giving Nash a chance to cash in his rain check.

She left by the door that opened onto the winding drive where her car was parked. She was thankful the auto club had managed to start it without taking it to the shop. The problem was she was postponing the inevitable, but when she contemplated major repairs like a new carburetor, the cost made her procrastinate.

The sky was a marbleized blue, streaked with orange. End-of-summer sunsets were her favorite. When she opened the door of her Datsun, she pulled out Nash's jacket, now laundered and folded, and threw her bag to the passenger's seat.

As she slammed the door and stepped back, she stomped on a foot and heard an "Ouch!"

She turned and found herself close enough to Nash to kiss him. Her erotic meter ran overtime. Flustered, she exploded, "That's what you get for sneaking up behind me."

Thrown off balance, Nash leaned against the car and balanced on one leg, rubbing his instep through his Docksiders. "I didn't sneak. You didn't hear me. You were too busy trying to leave without saying good-bye."

She pulled herself up to her full five feet five inches and said in a distancing tone, "I didn't think it was necessary."

"And I thought we'd established a . . . rapport."

They had. But she was going to ignore it. A cold wind blew around her heart. When would she be able to trust again? To forget John's divorce trial and the accusations his wife had made. To forget John had named Beth as co-respondent to get out of his marriage and change his life without regard for her reputation or feelings.

Nash dropped his foot and put his hand on her shoulder. "I just mean I thought we'd decided to be friendly rivals."

She stepped back, away from his touch. The spot he'd held was stinging with heat. "That's not a good idea."

He gave her a devastating smile. "What can it hurt?"

Her. Her creative streak. Her enthusiasm for the project. Her single-mindedness. Her heart. "I want Osgood's contract, Nash. At this moment, nothing is more important. If I want to be successful, I need it. I don't want to be distracted."

His eyes gleamed devilishly. "I'd be a distraction?"

A buzzing bee searched for nectar, leaves rustled with the gentle breeze, the truth rang in her ears. "You could be. Besides—"

"Besides what?"

She was afraid the fluttering pulse at her throat would give her attraction to him away. She wasn't ready to get involved with anyone. But to say that would be presumptuous when all he was asking for was friendship. "Nothing." She held out his jacket. "Thanks for letting me borrow this."

When he took it, his hand brushed hers. A reaction sparked in his eyes. Was he feeling the same chemistry she was?

The pause became uncomfortable. He looked at her closely and pushed a few tumbling curls away from her cheek. "Do you know how lovely you are?"

The tail of the question was low and husky. Tingles skipped along her cheek and her mouth went dry. "Nash . . ."

"I know. That's personal and you're all business. Do men believe the image you project?"

She noted how smoothly his jaw was shaved. Did he shave twice a day? Most men didn't. She'd bet he was a perfectionist. Corraling her thoughts, she said, "My image hasn't been a problem." At least it hadn't been until the story about her and John broke.

He didn't appear to believe her. "Are you seeing anyone now?"

"No. I don't want to." Uh-oh. That had slipped out.

He frowned. "Is that a generic disclaimer for all men or just me?"

How could he believe a woman wouldn't want to get

involved with him? Could he be that vulnerable? This conversation was entirely too serious. Time to lighten up. She smiled. "I plead the Fifth."

Before she changed her mind and accepted his offer of friendship or more, she slipped behind the wheel. "I really have to be leaving. Good luck on the project. I'll see you at the presentation."

Nash held the door, his eyes holding questions she wouldn't answer. Finally accepting her departure, he closed the door and stepped away. He watched as she started up the car. He was still watching as she drove away.

THREE

When Nash ventured into Plastics Unlimited, Osgood's parent company, he was struck anew by the architecture. He had toured the buildings two years ago. The style of the office complex was Spanish in design, yellow stucco accented by terra cotta and black wrought iron. It was unusual for this part of the country. The sprawling attached factory was similar, but one story instead of two. Nothing much had changed, including the smell of the small bakery that offered doughnuts and sandwiches. Most factories boasted a couple of microwaves and prepacked refrigerated lunch items. Not Osgood's domain.

The man's taste was eclectic to say the least, and Nash knew he'd have to employ more than one style in planning the resort. But he needed a unifying theme to tie it together. Maybe when he visited Osgood's resort in the Poconos this weekend, a good idea would grab him. If not, he'd work at it until he captured what he wanted.

Nash ambled down the carpeted hallway, noting the sconces and tastefully arranged wall decorations in black and gold. Remembering Osgood's office was situated at the end of the first-floor hall, he headed in that direction. He was surprised to find Osgood's secretary absent from her desk and the door to the inner sanctum only half closed.

Nash heard a sound he'd recognize anywhere—Beth's laugh. Her throaty laughter was sexy, and he wondered why he'd never thought of anyone's laughter in those terms before. Whenever she spoke, he expected a high, sweet voice to come out of her mouth. He was always surprised by a lilting alto. It reminded him of whipped cream on gingerbread—a mixture of rich and spicy.

She laughed again and he found himself moving closer. Why was she in Osgood's office? Was this a planned meeting or a spur-of-the-moment visit meant to take Osgood off guard? Despite what she'd said, maybe she was pursuing more than Osgood's contract. If so, Nash needed to find out.

"Can I tour the buildings or do I need a pass?" he heard her ask.

"I'll be your pass," Osgood answered. Nash thought he detected an undertone of smooth seduction. Was Beth attracted to older men with overused lines?

"I don't want to interrupt—"

"My dear, you aren't. Whatever's on my desk can wait. Being your escort will be much more enjoyable."

Over my dead body, Nash thought, barraged by an unexpected burst of jealousy he had no right to feel. Before he could rationally dismiss it, he pushed Osgood's office door open. "Good morning," he said cheerfully. "Your secretary wasn't at her desk." He turned to Beth and nodded. "We meet again."

Her dark-brown eyes widened when she saw him, then the black pupils narrowed. "Is this a coincidence?"

Nash shrugged. "Must be."

Osgood was scowling, as if Nash had interrupted when it was least convenient. The phone rang and Osgood picked it up, still glaring at Nash. His scowl deepened as he listened to the voice at the other end of the line. "I told you to take care of it. No, that won't do. I'm busy at the moment—"

"Mr. Osgood," Nash interrupted. "If you have matters that need your attention, I'll be glad to take Ms. Terrell on a tour of the facilities." He gave her what he thought was an ingenuous stare. "That *is* why you're here, isn't it?"

Beth ignored Nash. "I don't want to interfere with your schedule," she said to Osgood. "And if I don't feel Mr. Winchester is showing me everything there is to see, I'll be back to enlist your guidance."

Nash had to hand it to her. She was good at public relations, making Osgood feel important yet agreeing to Nash's suggestion. He took her elbow in his palm. "We won't bother stopping in before we leave. I'm sure you have more important concerns." Before Beth or Osgood could protest, Nash guided her out the door.

As soon as they were out of Osgood's sight and hearing, Beth pulled herself free of Nash's gentle grip. Her eyes blazed with anger. "What was *that* all about?"

Nash studied her with pretended casualness. Her Bambi-like eyes, usually so soft and friendly, were shooting gold sparks. Together with the tousled devil-may-care hairdo, the turned-up tip of her nose, the delicately pointed chin. . . . His body heated up. It was an enjoyable sensation, one that had been a stranger the past few years. He'd thought he'd outgrown raging hormones. The idea that he hadn't and that this woman invoked them excited him.

He smiled. "That was about me taking you on a tour. I was a sightseeing guide at Gettysburg one summer. I won't let you miss anything." He took a step forward but she didn't budge.

She waved her hand in agitation. "You just blew a perfectly good opportunity for me to get to know him better."

Before he could cork it, the question spurted out. "How well do you want to get to know him?"

"Damn it, Nash. I told you before. I don't care about him. I want his contract. Why won't you believe me?"

He felt his cheeks flush and the nerve in his jaw jump. He wanted to reach out to her soft cheek and soothe her anger away. The fire coursing through him whenever he looked at her made him want to take her to bed. Knowing her had become all important . . . compulsive. And he was afraid it was clouding his judgment.

But he felt he owed her an explanation. "Two years ago I worked my tail off for an Osgood project. I didn't get it because the other architect he chose was a woman who inveigled her way into Osgood's bed."

Beth appeared shocked for a moment but recovered quickly and glared at him. "You have a colossal ego! Maybe her work was better than yours. Is that so inconceivable?"

He kept his temper at a slow boil and wondered why it was so important for Beth to believe him. "I know better. She wasn't finished with her boards the day of the presentation. And after she was awarded the project, he had to bring in another architect to consult because she hadn't thought through the designs accurately."

He could see Beth was torn between the desire to defend her sex and the desire to believe him. "I don't lie, Beth. And I don't contribute to rumor. I'm giving you the facts. There's proof if you want that, too."

Her expression changed, becoming less accusing. "If that's true, your anger's justified. But I don't lie, either,

Nash. I'm not interested in an entanglement with Osgood.''

He wished he could search her heart because he longed to believe her, to believe she was incapable of ruthlessness and manipulation. ''Then I guess you're here for the same reason I am.''

She examined him closely. ''If you mean I'm here to figure out Osgood's taste, you're right.''

He checked out her mint-green slacks, silk blouse, and flat shoes, convincing himself she was telling the truth. ''Then let's walk the grounds. They're lovely.''

After a long, probing stare, she nodded and followed him through the back entrance into a grassy area with white birches interspersed with park benches. Trying to get back on an amiable footing, she commented on the restful atmosphere.

''Osgood treats his employees well. He feels if they're happy, they're more productive,'' Nash added.

They crossed a stone bridge stretching over a narrow stream and stood at its apex. Nash turned his back on the scenery to face Beth. He was about to do something incredibly smart, or incredibly stupid. He wasn't sure which. He simply knew he had to do it.

Watching the sun flicker on Beth's round gold earrings, he asked, ''I suppose you're going to inspect Osgood's resort in the Poconos?''

She looked as if he'd guessed every card in her poker hand. He saw the debate going on inside her as she decided whether or not to tell him her plans. Finally, she sighed and admitted, ''This weekend.''

He was right on the mark. ''So am I. Why don't we drive up together and save gas?''

Beth hung the strapless royal-blue taffeta dress in the double-width closet. She must be crazy! How did she end up in the Poconos with Nash Winchester? Couldn't she learn to be rational instead of impulsive? Apparently not.

Damn the man's smile. Damn his sexiness and warmth and especially his logic. The logic had snared her. She remembered his words. "We're going to be there from Saturday to Sunday. We might as well drive up together and meet for dinner."

Although her car hadn't left her stranded again, it now not only chugged in damp weather but whenever she let it idle. Riding here with Nash had seemed like a practical idea. But since when had practicality been one of her virtues? A dinner engagement hadn't seemed threatening . . . then. What had possessed her to buy this dress? It was the popular shorter style with a layered skirt. But now when she looked at it, it seemed . . . skimpy. Time enough to worry about that later.

She gave the sketch pad on the desk a longing stare. She and Nash had gone their separate ways in the morning after they'd arrived. As she canvassed the grounds, sketching and jotting down ideas, she'd come up with a wonderful plan. She'd noticed the different age groups swimming, walking, jogging, and participating in sports. What if she used the concept of playgrounds, one for each particular population?

She could envision a maze with corners and insets and arches and flowers where lovers could chase each other and kiss. There'd be a section for children with boulders to scramble over, ladders to climb, old-fashioned swings made of tires, and a sunken sandbox. She could picture an area for athletes—an obstacle course surrounded by a track, a quiet garden with benches for seniors, hedge sculptures, a stream with a covered bridge. And finally, a nature trail that everyone could enjoy.

Picture after picture tumbled one over the other in her mind and her fingers itched to make preliminary drawings. But that would have to wait. There'd been a note on her door when she returned to the room. From Nash. "If you'd like to play tennis, meet me at 2:30 at the pro shop. We can rent racquets. Hope to see you there."

She'd told herself she was going because she needed the exercise, but her subconscious knew better. The strength of Nash's personality drew her, as did his honesty. Losing a project to a woman under the circumstances he'd explained had to be a professional blow, one a man might not easily admit. Nash could admit it and she admired that. She also wanted to tentatively explore the sexual feelings he aroused that were at the same time exciting and frightening.

She grabbed her room key from the dresser, stuffed it in her pocket, and locked her door. The sun played peek-a-boo with marshmallowlike clouds as she walked to the courts. The temperature in the Poconos was fifteen degrees cooler than in Lancaster. Seventy degrees was a welcome respite, a perfect day for tennis.

Nash was waiting on the court side of the shop, two racquets in hand. His hair-covered legs were bronze against white shorts. She felt as though she'd just run a marathon rather than walked the short distance from her room.

To give herself time to quiet her thudding pulse, she teased, "You were sure I was coming?"

He shrugged. "I was hoping. But if you didn't, I could have found a partner."

Beth's eyes migrated to a group of women seated at a round table under an umbrella. The thought of Nash playing tennis with one of them instead of her made her stomach tighten. "Blonde or brunette?" she asked flippantly.

He wrapped one of her curls around his forefinger.

"I'm partial to chestnut. Did you know your red high-lights glow like fire in the sun?"

Unnerved by the feel of his finger in her hair, she turned to the courts. "They're full."

Nash pointed to the far court on the left. "See that couple? They said if you showed, they'd like to play doubles. Are you game?"

When he smiled, a small dimple appeared on his cheek. The desire to touch it was strong enough to make her curl her fingers into her palm. "I might dis-grace you. I haven't played tennis in a couple of years."

"You couldn't disgrace anyone."

Admiration shone in his eyes and she wondered if it would still be there if he knew about the scandal. "You don't know me, Nash."

"I want to remedy that."

His eyes were too green, too dark, too inviting. Shaking off their embracing quality, she forced a laugh. "I'll let you know one thing. I used to have a wicked backhand."

He playfully chucked her chin. "Then let's go get 'em, tiger." When he hooked a strong, muscular arm around her shoulders, her knees felt like wet noodles. How was she going to play tennis?

Shaking hands with the couple and setting up a few guidelines put her mind on the game. From the first serve, playing tennis with Nash was exhilarating. She took the net; he played back. His long, powerful volleys complemented her short, quick strokes. Their opponents played well, but Nash and Beth won the match.

After the spike that won them the final point, Nash rushed toward Beth and gave her a bear hug. "You were great."

Every nerve ending tingled; all her senses were fully alive. Enfolded in his arms she felt aroused, womanly

. . . safe. She steadied the tremor in her voice. "You were no slouch, either."

He leaned back, sliding his large, hot hands down her shoulders to her elbows. "But I had a better view of you than you had of me."

She remembered stooping over for the ball, losing her balance, stretching into unladylike positions. "You want a rematch so *I* can take unfair advantage?"

"Would you do that to me?" He leered, obviously not thinking about tennis.

She waggled her finger at his chest. "You have a vivid imagination."

"Would you like me to tell you exactly how vivid it is?"

The question was teasing, but his smoky voice was rife with sexual vibrations. Her pulse raced, her breathing turned shallow, her tongue stuck to the roof of her mouth. She unplastered it, broke her gaze from his, and glanced over his shoulder. "Our opponents want to congratulate us."

He looked disappointed the private moment was gone. With a wry grin, he dropped his arms. "We should buy them a drink."

This man could easily become addictive. She took the safe route. "I really should pass. I have ideas I'd like to get on paper before I forget them."

"Are you running again or are you telling me work comes first?"

She was a free agent. She didn't owe him any explanations, but she didn't want to be rude, either. "Work comes first . . . sometimes. I work in spurts and spells. If I sit down and attempt to force ideas, I turn out trash." That was true. She worked best when her personal muse was on the job.

"And the running?"

Did he always cut to the heart and see through the

camouflage? "Nash, you're imagining things. I'm having dinner with you, aren't I?"

His green eyes bored into hers. "You are."

Obviously he was trying to interpret what she was thinking and feeling. She ended the discussion. "What time should I meet you?"

"I'll pick you up at your door at eight."

She suspected when he took a woman out, he called the shots. She'd let him call this one . . . this time. "Eight it is."

Nash rapped on the door firmly and adjusted his tie. He thought he'd get to know Beth better this weekend, but she wasn't helping him out except for brief flashes when her guard was down. Although she'd chattered during the drive to the mountains, she hadn't revealed where she was born or where she grew up. She'd focused mainly on her college experiences and her life in Lancaster. Maybe he could discover more details over dinner. At this point, he didn't know if he wanted more information for business reasons or personal ones. His personal interest was stretching beyond usual bounds.

When she opened the door, Nash felt a rush of adrenaline speed through him. "Wow!"

She blushed and fingered the strand of pearls at her neck. Matching pearl studs adorned her ears, and two pearl combs anchored her curls away from her temples. Her eyes toured down Nash's charcoal suit and he felt his body respond.

Their gazes connected for a moment before she broke the tension. "Come on in. I just have to get my shawl. Is it cold out? I forgot the temperature here drops at night."

She was chattering again. There was no doubt in his mind that she felt the pull between them and was doing everything in her power to circumvent it. When she picked up her purse at the dresser, he took the black velvet shawl from the desk chair and held it around her arms. Seeing him in the mirror, she backed up so he could drop it over her shoulders. But he didn't drop it.

Nash couldn't help letting his fingers lift her ringlets in the back. They were as soft as a kitten's fur, silky, and he breathed in either her shampoo or perfume. Whatever it was, the scent was captivating, slightly floral yet mysterious. His fingertips lightly brushed the nape of her neck and he experienced a jolt of desire made more powerful because of her shiver. When he found her eyes in the mirror, he knew she wasn't repulsed or afraid. She was excited. Her guard had dropped.

Only for a moment. She crossed the ends of the shawl over her breasts and murmured, "Thank you." Angling wide around the corner of the king-size bed, she stood at the door and waited.

In silence, they walked under the wisteria-covered trellis to the dining room. The hostess guided them to a table for two. Before Nash could help, Beth removed her shawl, laid it over the back of the chair, and sat down.

He swore to himself. He wanted to make her comfortable, not nervous. After the waiter took their order, Nash asked if she'd gotten much work done.

Her eyes sparkled as brilliantly as the hurricane lamps and the crystal chandeliers. "A good bit. I worked straight through and was almost late getting dressed."

Her passion for her work pleased him but distracted him, too. Was she equally as passionate when she made love? He turned off the fantasy. "You're serious about working when the mood hits."

She picked up the rose linen napkin and spread it on her lap. "Absolutely. Like my dad says, you've got to buy when there's a sale.'' At Nash's puzzled look, she explained: ''His version of make hay while the sun shines.''

Nash chuckled. ''I see. But what do you do if it rains, the deadline's approaching, and you're blocked?''

''I do something to get unblocked. I jog and let my mind imagine one scene after another, I sort through my favorite landscaping books, I meditate.''

''Meditate?''

''Sure. I think about my client and his needs, visualize colors, and let the terrain fill in.''

This woman fascinated him. She was intelligent and sassy, with a stroke of innocence thrown in. ''We work in totally different ways.''

She laughed and tilted her head. ''You didn't work this afternoon?''

He wondered if she knew how absolutely enchanting she could be. ''I worked out in the gym.''

''After a game of tennis?''

''That's usually what I do Saturday afternoons. I've found that a schedule helps life flow more smoothly.''

She shook her head and her curly hair teased her neck. ''Schedules are limiting.''

''Schedules increase productivity.''

''I'm *very* productive.''

''Maybe you can teach me your secret.'' He'd always wanted to learn to be more flexible without letting anything suffer.

She bypassed his suggestion. ''What do you do if you feel like going . . . shopping on a Saturday afternoon?'' At his expression she said, ''Sorry. Bad choice. What if you feel like . . . horseback riding?''

''I work out first.''

Her foot tapped his shin as she crossed her legs. ''I suppose your office hours are sacred?''

"I try to stick to them." He shrugged. "It helps to keep my life compartmentalized."

She looked disconcerted. "You plan Sundays, too?"

He felt as if he was taking an oral exam and failing. "I usually spend part of them with Shannon and her family."

She shook her head as if his method was either unbelievable or impractical. "Don't you get bored?"

His schedule kept him from getting lonely. He was too busy most of the time to notice it. Except lately. Especially since he'd met Beth and realized something was missing from his life. Joy and intimacy. "Boredom isn't one of my problems."

"How do you get your ideas?"

"I take notes, study specifications, analyze, and start sketching."

"What happens if *you* get blocked?"

"I don't. I go back to my notes and work through it. If one sketch doesn't work, I begin another."

She frowned. "It seems a waste to me."

"I disagree. The ideas I discard, I can pull out of the file and use later."

"You *are* organized."

She made it sound as if organization was an albatross around his neck. "Is that a crime?"

Reflectively fingering the mum in the vase on the table, she admitted, "No. But my mom's tried to teach me to be like you all my life and it doesn't work for me. She can't understand that I'm organized in my own way. Now Pops understands."

Finally. She was going to give him some background. "That's your dad?"

"Uh-hm."

Keep it light. Don't sound too interested. "What's he do?"

She watched Nash very closely. "He owns a tavern."

Nash was aware her chin lifted as she dared him to make a condescending remark. "Does he tend bar, too, or just manage?"

"He tends bar some evenings," she said warily. "He likes people."

Nash wondered if her friends or acquaintances had put her or her father down because of his occupation. "Bartenders know how to listen. They give good advice, too, because they know human nature."

She seemed surprised by his understanding. "Do you hang around bars often? You seem to know what goes on there."

"I used to. Started when I was twelve." Why had he said that? To shock her? To get her interested in his life?

Beth hid any astonishment she might be feeling. "Can you tell me why?"

"I knew all the bartenders in our section of town in case I needed to find our father." She was waiting for more. He shouldn't have started this; he'd only ever talked about it to Shannon. "Dad liked to rub elbows with his buddies in bars rather than working."

"That must have been hard on you."

"It was hard on Mom. But she held us together." His voice held nothing but admiration and respect for his mother. Her life had been hard, but she'd never crumbled.

After Beth absorbed the information, she asked, "Is Shannon older or younger than you?"

"Older, but only by two years. It's always seemed as if we're the same age. When Dad left for good, she took it harder than I did."

"How old were you?"

Nash was pleased Beth was interested enough to continue asking questions. "Sixteen." As he studied her face, he didn't see pity in her eyes, just empathy.

"Where's your mother now?"

Sadness crawled across Nash's heart. "She died a year after I graduated from college."

Beth looked embarrassed. "I'm sorry."

He leaned forward, resting his arm on the edge of the table. "It's okay. It's been a long time. The doctors said she had a stroke, but Shan and I think she died of a broken heart."

"You've known a lot of loss."

When Christy died, he thought he'd never get over it, but memories brought strength as well as sorrow. "A lot of good times, too. I don't think about the bad ones." He took the risk of being honest with her. "I don't usually talk about this."

She reached out and touched his hand. "I'm glad you did. I had the impression you were . . . larger than life. Too successful to have problems like the rest of us."

He turned his hand palm up and clasped her fingers. "I'm not so different from you."

"Pops always taught me people were more alike than different. I guess I forgot."

"Where is his tavern?"

"Virginia," she said quickly, pulling her hand back. She picked up her glass of water garnished with a slice of lemon and took a sip. A moment later she nodded to the side of the room. "Here comes our dinner."

Nash knew the serious conversation was over for now, but he felt he'd made at least a modicum of progress. He was also certain she wasn't simply nervous. She was hiding something. What?

As they ate, Beth felt as if she were being surrounded by a sensual net she couldn't escape. Nash had a powerful appeal that was bowling her over. He was strong yet gentle, sexy yet caring. An inviting combination.

She was beginning to convince herself a friendship between them might be possible.

He was a good conversationalist and time flew. Since he didn't ask any more background questions, she relaxed and let the conversation flow from tastes in music and art, to some of his projects and a few of hers. The food was superb, the candlelight romantic. When her knee grazed his, her stomach flipped. They sat talking long after they'd finished a third cup of coffee.

At a lull Nash leaned back in his chair. "Would you like to dance?"

A warning alarm buzzed in Beth's mind. She pretended she didn't hear it. "Sure."

His hand rested protectively in the small of her back as he guided her to the wooden dance floor. That she could handle, but she knew she had a problem when he took her in his arms. His hold was light and easy.

She didn't feel light and easy or as if she wanted him to be merely a friend. Avoiding his eyes, she looked over his shoulder. The dance floor became more crowded and Nash gently tightened his hold and maneuvered them away from a collision. Beth was overtaken by the awareness that she liked being in Nash's arms, liked his warmth against hers, liked everything about him. But she wasn't ready for a relationship. She wasn't ready to let personal feelings interfere with her work. The timing was all wrong.

Nash didn't seem to think so. "You dance well," he murmured at her temple.

"You're easy to follow." She made the mistake of looking at him.

He brought their hands from the ballroom position into his chest. "Are you enjoying yourself?"

Her hand was enclosed by his fingers and his suit coat. The competing textures confused her nervous system as her eyes focused on his lips. Firm, well-shaped, masculine lips—

"Beth?"

Apparently she'd missed his question. "I'm sorry. What?"

She felt his slow smile in her bones. "Are you glad you came?"

"Yes." She heard her breathlessness and knew he heard it, too.

His hand went to the back of her neck and her world tilted. With slight pressure he nudged her head onto his shoulder and rubbed his chin against her cheek. She felt his heart accelerate and was sure hers matched its pace. A tautness invaded Nash's body. She could tell by the slight stiffening of his arms and upper body. Instead of pressing into her, he held himself away. She had a good idea why and his restraint excited her. She closed her eyes and imagined lying naked in his arms.

Another couple bumped them and Beth's thighs pushed against Nash's. His arousal scorched her and she held her breath, afraid to move.

Nash shifted slightly to separate them but didn't loosen his hold. When the song ended, Beth opened her eyes, feeling as if she'd been buried in an avalanche. It took her a moment to realize they were standing still.

As she raised her head, Nash said, "The band's taking a break. Would you like to wait or go back to your room?"

How was she going to extricate herself from this one? If they continued dancing, she feared where it would lead. If she said she wanted to go back, would he misconstrue that as an invitation? One crossroad at a time.

"I'd like to go back."

When they returned to the table, Beth insisted on

paying her share of the check. Unlike some other men she'd dated, Nash didn't argue.

As they walked back to her room, Beth gazed at the stars. It was a night for sharing, for spending time with someone you loved. Now where had *that* thought come from? She shivered. Although her shawl protected her, she missed the warmth of Nash's arms. He hadn't touched her since they stopped dancing.

At the door to her room, he stared at her for a long moment but kept his arms at his sides. "I had a nice evening."

"Me, too."

Stepping closer, he lifted her chin with his knuckle. Excitement bubbled inside her as she held her breath, sure he was going to kiss her.

He gave her a tender smile. "Would you like to go for a jog?"

FOUR

"Now?" Beth asked in a bewildered tone.

"Now."

Not kissing Beth Terrell had taken more willpower than Nash had had to exercise in quite a while. Afraid he'd scare her away, he'd backed off. But he didn't want to say good night. A jog might help the sexual tension in his body yet keep him in her company. He hoped his bum knee could handle a little more punishment without giving him trouble. Tennis this afternoon had really done him in, but he'd wanted to spend time with her.

Seeing that she looked disappointed and confused by his question, he added, "I have trouble sleeping in strange beds. A jog before I turn in tires me out enough so I close my eyes and forget where I am."

He watched her swallow hard. Was she imagining them together in said bed?

"I'd, uh, have to change."

He grinned. She was adorable when she was flustered. "I hope so. Will ten minutes do it? I'll meet you at the office. The path around the parking lot's well lit. We can use that."

* * *

Beth slammed shut the dresser drawer. Holding up her pale-blue jogging pants in front of her, she wished she'd sent them to a dump and bought a new pair. They were limp from hundreds of washings. The sweatshirt wasn't much better. She sighed as she unzipped her dress. Nash was about to see another side of her. The side that liked to be comfortable and didn't give a hoot about fashion.

She sighed again. Nash. Did she want him to kiss her or not? She had a feeling a kiss could have led them straight to a strange bed. Yet she was aching to find out if the chemistry between them was as potent as it seemed.

He was waiting for her in front of the office in the same white shorts he'd worn for tennis. The red T-shirt was fresh. She loved the way it hinted at the muscles underneath and pulled slightly across his shoulders. As the breeze swept by, she couldn't tell if the earthy musk scent belonged to the summer night or him.

He reached out and ran his fingertips over one comb in her hair. "You might lose these." There was a sexy catch in his voice.

Instinct urged her to rub her head against his hand, but she resisted. "I forgot to take them out. Now I don't have anywhere to put them."

He didn't move away. "Where's your key?"

Thinking about exactly where it was turned her cheeks crimson. "Uh . . . it's in my bra."

His eyes were twinkling and the corner of his mouth curved up, but he suppressed the smile. In a brisk businesslike manner, he unfastened one pearl barrette at a time. "I have a pocket."

With interest she watched his hands go to his waistband. Sucking in his breath, he found the small pocket, inserted the barrettes, and buttoned it. It disappeared under his shirt and she could picture it flat against his stomach, right above dark-brown hair and . . .

She quickly bent down and went into her stretching routine. What kind of power did this man have over her that she couldn't look at him without being overcome by sexual desire? This had never happened with other men. Certainly never with John, even though they'd been emotionally close. And it had nothing to do with John being twenty years older. There'd been friendship between them, caring, confidentiality . . . so she'd thought. That's why his selfishness and betrayal had hurt so badly.

Nash stretched, too, and it was difficult keeping her eyes away from his long legs, the biceps, his angular face. When he looked at her and asked if she was ready, she realized what a good idea this had been. She couldn't wait to run off the disruptive feelings he initiated.

The mountain air was devoid of truck fumes, clatter, humidity. It whistled in her ears, cleansed her lungs, warned her she was breathing the same air as Nash, and he was merely a foot away. He matched his speed to hers and she wondered what he could really do if he let himself go.

"Is the pace all right?" he asked.

"Fine. How often do you jog?"

"Three or four times a week. You?"

"The same. Where do you go?"

"The track at the high school."

She should have guessed he'd pick someplace routine, nondistracting.

He glanced at her out of the corner of his eye. "I suppose you prefer the streets and scenery?"

She laughed. "Bingo."

They'd run a half mile when they rounded a corner of the parking lot. Nash faltered as they curved, and his hands hit the macadam. Pain marked his face when he fell on his backside and stretched out his left leg in front of him.

It took a moment for Beth to realize what had happened. The prolific oaths that came out of his mouth told her this wasn't minor. She caught her breath and knelt beside him. "What happened?"

He swore again. "I pushed it. I should've known after that game of tennis the knee would give out—" He winced, leaned back on his hands and pressed his eyes shut. "Give me a minute."

"Has this happened before?"

His eyes flew open and he nodded.

"Is it locked?"

Another nod.

She took hold of his leg below the knee and with her thumb and forefinger pressed on either side, ignoring the heat from the skin and the teasing texture of the soft brown hair. He didn't react to the pressure, so she knew she wasn't causing more distress. Abruptly, he contracted the muscles and jerked the joint.

"That's it," he said with relief as something seemed to slip into place and his face relaxed.

She sank back on her heels. "Does this happen often?"

The lines across his forehead and around his mouth eased. "No, thank God. I can usually tell when it's strained and ready to go. I knew I was pushing it."

"Why did you?"

He didn't answer immediately. His chest rose and fell a few times before he said, "Because jogging seemed more prudent than kissing you."

Her pulse sped up and she took a deep breath. She was startled by his scent. His aura of masculinity surrounded her. "Can you move it? You don't want it to stiffen up."

The desire in his eyes made her blush as he let her off the hook. "How do you know so much about knees?"

"Mom's a nurse."

He bent his leg stiffly and pushed himself to a sitting position. "A few hours of ice and it'll be good as new."

She rose up on her knees and planted her hands on her hips. "It'll be sore tomorrow and you know it."

"You won't let me pull a macho act and suffer in silence?"

"I never could understand what Mom saw in John Wayne."

"Sharing thoughts and feelings is more difficult for men than women." Before she could debate the issue, he added, "That's not chauvinistic. I know from experience." He climbed to his feet, favoring the injured knee. He brushed his hands together, wiping off the dirt and small pieces of gravel.

Beth scrambled up, and before she thought better of it, grasped his hand and turned it over to examine his palm. She gently rubbed her thumb along an abrasion under his forefinger. "This could get nasty if you don't get the grime out. Do you have peroxide?"

He was gazing at her strangely as if he were in pain, but not the same kind of pain he had experienced when he fell. "I have a first-aid kit in the car." His voice was low and husky.

She realized she didn't want to let go of his hand and traced her thumb along his lifeline.

"Beth—"

The green glints in his gaze had nothing to do with the overhead lights. Desire strong enough to make her body steam rushed through her. Was this attraction to Nash real? Was her liking for him misplaced? Could she trust him without getting hurt? The questions seemed inconsequential at the moment as his eyes touched her like searing hands pulling her closer. He inspired feelings and sensations she never knew existed.

His arms came around her and when he bent his head, she raised hers to meet him. There was no shyness, no simple friendship, no rivalry. As their lips touched, everything between them changed. Nash's passion was hot on her lips. She'd never felt that kind of heat before, mingled with need, so much need. She wanted to give him everything he needed.

After a tentative search, his tongue pushed forward seeking her response. Hers returned his thrusts with the same vehemence until she was caught in a cyclone of spiraling sensations. The kiss was everything perfect—sunrise at the beach, a Monet painting, children's laughter. It was as exciting as lightning, as frightening as thunder, as wonderful as Christmas. So many conflicting feelings—need, curiosity, her desire to experience more. She framed his jaw with her hands and caressed his cheeks.

He groaned and his hands answered her ministrations with eager exploration up and down her back. Each pass became slower, more tactile, more provocative. Her body was yielding to him and she sensed his longing to touch her more intimately. His hands slipped under her top and kneaded her damp skin. She pushed into him and knew the strength of his arousal. With the same abandon that was driving her, he rubbed against her to pleasure them both.

Tearing his lips from hers, he moaned, "God, Beth. You're so soft, so giving."

The word registered. Giving. Yes, she was giving. Too giving. What was she doing? Giving had gotten her into trouble before. Giving passion was much more dangerous and complicated than giving *com*passion. She froze and went still.

His arms dropped and she heard the long, slow wail of a train whistle in the distance. She shivered from air suddenly gone cold.

Nash put at least six inches between them. The muscle in his jaw tensed as his eyes grew opaque. "I'm sorry if you didn't want that. I read the signals wrong."

She couldn't let him take full responsibility. "You read them correctly. But after we started . . ."

"You had second thoughts."

His low voice in the dark night sent a chill up her spine. "Something like that." Why did she feel as though she'd hurt him? It was only a kiss for heaven's sake! He looked paler. Was it from restraining his passion? Not pushing her farther than she wanted to go?

"Thank you for stopping."

He looked perplexed. "It's what you wanted."

"Yes, I know. But some men consider their needs first."

"When a woman says no, she means no."

Beth searched his face for underlying feelings. "I didn't say it."

"Not out loud, but you said it. I'd like to know why."

She sorted through her reactions quickly, concealing the most important reason. "First of all, because we're bidding on the same project. I'm not even sure you believe I'm not after Osgood."

"And second?"

"I don't want to get involved."

"That's not an explanation." The look in his eyes was heart-stopping.

She protected herself. "I don't owe you an explanation."

His stance became defensive, his shoulders rigid, his arms stiff at his sides. "No, I guess you don't." He turned away from her and looked at the hotel. "We'd better start back. It'll take longer than it did to get here.''

Nash felt stilted and wooden as he avoided temptation and kept his eyes in front of him. Normal male urges were no surprise, but the intensity of this one in response to Beth's kiss was. She walked quietly beside him as awkwardness settled around them like a fog. Her rejection had hurt. Just like Monica's had. After Christy died, his wife couldn't touch him, couldn't let him touch her. Lack of physical intimacy had led to lack of communication and eventually separate lives.

Hazarding a glance at Beth, Nash still felt an ache inside. She was so touchable, with a figure that matched her friendliness. It wasn't stick-stiff or model-thin, but huggable and womanly. Her breasts were small but full, her stomach flat but soft, her hips pleasantly rounded. And her mouth? More than friendly. Sensual, taking, giving, making him long to bury himself in her.

He wasn't comfortable with the desires and emotions she aroused. Was he out of practice? No. He'd dated on and off over the past few years. But nothing had been more important than Shannon and her family, and work, and his exercise regimen. Beth shook him up and put other concerns in the background. Her reticence added to her allure. It wasn't coy or fake. It made him look at himself critically and ask himself what he wanted.

He wasn't sure yet so he didn't know whether to push harder to discover what was behind her rejection. Contrary to what she said, she might have designs on Osgood and some sense of morality wouldn't let her get involved with Nash. Lord, he hoped that wasn't true. If it was . . .

The best thing to do was to stay away from her. The hell of it was, he didn't want to.

*   *   *

Monday afternoon, Beth sat with a group of architects and contractors at a builders' luncheon. Always on the lookout for business, she usually enjoyed mingling. Today she was distracted and had done more daydreaming than mingling. At least Nash wasn't here. After his mind-bending kiss, he'd withdrawn. The walk back to her hotel room had been tense, the drive home polite and strained. They'd lost their camaraderie and she missed it, more than she was willing to admit.

Tom Rosenthal tapped her on the shoulder and took the vacant seat next to her. "Good to see you here."

"You, too," she said politely. Rosenthal had never singled her out before and she wondered why he had now. Maybe because they both had designs on Osgood's resort.

He studied her closely and seemed to weigh his words when he spoke. "I see you at these shindigs whenever they're planned. It's funny Winchester doesn't have to lobby as much as we do. He's never here."

"Maybe he has more work than he can handle."

"Yeah, all the big jobs. I'd sure like a few of them, but Winchester's beaten me out of most of them. And I don't think it's all hard work that's done it." He sounded bitter.

"I don't understand."

Rosenthal rubbed his palms on his knees. "Look, you're new around here."

What did that have to do with anything? "I've been here three years."

"Yeah, but have you had to compete against Winchester before?"

Most of her work had been with clients landscaping private homes. "No."

A victorious look came into his eyes. "That's what I thought. You don't know how sly he is."

Sly was never a word she'd associate with Nash. "Would you explain?"

Rosenthal seemed to be filled with nervous energy. He couldn't sit still. He slid to the edge of the cushion. "When Winchester first came to this area, he invited me to lunch. He's done the same with other architects."

"I don't see the harm in that. Colleagues getting together . . ."

Rosenthal snorted. "He digs. He tries to learn everything he can about you so he can use it against you."

"Blackmail?" Her voice squeaked.

"Not exactly. But if he learns something damaging, he leaks it to the client. That must be how he's won projects away from me. I had a drinking problem a few years back. I believe he told the clients and it swayed the vote."

She couldn't believe that about Nash. She didn't *want* to believe that about Nash. "He certainly didn't learn that over lunch unless you confided in him."

"No, I didn't. I've heard he uses a private investigator."

Beth had had her fill of private investigators. The one John Winston's ex-wife had hired had only cared about getting paid for his photographs, not the truth behind them. "From whom did you hear this?"

He impatiently waved his hand. "You don't believe in gossip. That's fine. But where there's smoke, there's fire. I heard when Winchester was bidding on those million-dollar amusement parks, he looked into everybody's background."

She played devil's advocate. "That doesn't mean he found anything or used what he found."

"Don't be naive, Ms. Terrell. He didn't get famous by accident."

The angry tilt of Rosenthal's mouth made her wary. "He has talent."

"Yes, he does. But so do a score of others."

"Why are you telling me this?"

"Because you should be forewarned so you can watch your back. You and Winchester seemed to be getting cozy at Osgood's. His interest might not be what it seems. Even though you *are* an attractive young woman."

His compliment somehow seemed uncomplimentary. "I still don't understand. Telling me won't help you."

"Let's just say if I can't get Osgood's resort, I'd rather not see Winchester get it, either." He stood, and with a lift of his hand, moved to a group of men on the far side of the room.

Beth stared at her water glass. *Had* she been naive again? Was Nash's character different from what it seemed? Was his "honesty" a calculated ruse to learn something about her he could use against her? The question that nagged the most was: had the kiss been part of a ploy or real?

By Saturday morning, Beth had decided Nash Winchester was not a part of her life; therefore, she didn't need to worry about his business tactics. Not unless he unearthed the scandal and somehow put her in low regard with Osgood. Maybe she should tell Osgood herself. No. That could be a bad move.

To keep her mind from wandering to Nash or Osgood, she went to the paint store and bought everything she needed to redo her living-room walls. She wanted to change the cantaloupe color to pale yellow and paint the ceiling sky blue with white puffy clouds. The change would brighten up the apartment for fall and winter.

After she moved the furniture and covered it, she began with the ceiling. She tackled a wall next until the blue dried. While she sponged on the clouds, a headache began to pound at her temples. Early afternoon became late afternoon, and crawling up and down the ladder became tougher and tougher. As she worked on the third wall, she felt light-headed.

The doorbell rang. Laying her roller in the paint tray, she shook her head to clear it and went to the door.

Nash stood on the other side of the screen in a black polo shirt and denim cut-offs. "May I come in?"

Instantly, just from seeing him, she again felt his mouth on hers, the heat of his embrace, the intensity of his passion. Recognition shone in his eyes. He remembered, too. Her runaway pulse added to her bout of dizziness.

She looked down at her faded red camisole top and the orange knit shorts spattered with paint. Flicking off the kerchief that protected her hair, she said, "You don't want to set foot in there. I'm in the middle of something."

"I brought your barrettes. I thought you might need them." He held out his hand.

She opened the screen door and took them from him. When her finger touched his hand, she felt a shock of awareness, remembering her thumb moving over his palm, the feel of his jaw beneath her hands.

"Beth, what's wrong? It's eighty-five degrees and your fingers are like ice!"

She put her hand to her forehead and rubbed across her brow. "I have a crummy headache and I feel a little dizzy. Maybe it's the flu."

He sniffed. "What are you doing in there?"

She looked down at her clothes. "What does it look like I'm doing?"

He pulled her out the door and pushed her down on the top step. "Sit and take deep breaths. What kind of paint are you using?"

She raised her head marginally so it wouldn't spin. "I don't know. It was on sale. Why?"

"You're getting poisoned by the fumes. Maybe you're just sensitive to them. Some people are."

"The windows are open."

He stood. "I'll get you a chair so you're more comfortable."

"I have one more wall to finish."

"I don't want you going back in there." His stare nailed her to the step.

Rebelliousness surfaced and pushed her unsteadily to her feet. "I decide what I do. Not you."

"Beth, be reasonable. Do you want to feel worse than you do now?"

"Of course not. But I want to finish."

The stern expression on his face gentled. "Will you agree to sit on a chair on the porch if I finish it?"

"You can't do that. You'll get paint all over you."

"Maybe I'm not as messy as you." At her glare, he teased, "That was a joke. See? The fumes have made you lose your sense of humor. That's serious."

He looked so smug, so masculine, and so wonderful. "Why do you want to do this?"

"Because you need help. And if I don't do it, you'll go charging back in there."

His lips were so sensual. They'd been firm, hot . . . The paint *had* gone to her head. "I'm sure you have more profitable things to do."

"Maybe. But this won't take long."

"I'll pay you."

"Beth—"

"You name the price or no deal."

His eyes twinkled merrily. "After I'm finished, I'll tell you what my work's worth. Agreed?"

The racket in her head made thinking difficult. "Agreed."

While he went to get a chair, she stared down at the two barrettes in her hand.

Nash peeked under the sheets to find out what kind of furniture coordinated with a blue sky and yellow walls. He'd carried a blue platform rocker outside. Lifting the sheet covering the sofa, he found rainbow upholstery, each color of the spectrum muted into the next. One hulking form drew his attention because he had no idea what it was. He laughed out loud when he pulled off the cover. It was a swing chair! The child in Beth lurked not far below the surface. He'd like to rediscover that aspect of his own personality.

Plastic crackled under his feet as he found the paint tray. This wasn't what he'd expected to do today. Despite his resolve to stay away from Beth, he'd found he couldn't stop thinking about her. Fantasizing about her. The excitement and arousal he experienced whenever she invaded his mind shook him. When he'd found the barrettes, he'd followed the nagging inclination to see her again. Just a short visit. To test the waters. To reconnect. To convince himself that seeing her wasn't as important as he'd imagined. After he'd dropped her off on Sunday and entered his house, he'd felt . . . lonely. The silence that had once been friendly seemed to shout angrily at him. Maybe it was a wise voice in his heart telling him to forget the past and get on with his future.

He didn't know why but it had taken courage to appear on her doorstep. Since when had he felt unsure about seeing a woman? Since he'd met Beth Terrell. Her smile caused his nervous system to engage in gymnastics.

Trying to forget Beth was sitting on her front porch, dressed in clothes that molded to her body like a glove to a hand, he lifted the roller from the tray and picked up where she'd left off.

An hour later Nash stood bare-chested in the middle of the room and swiped at his sweaty forehead with the back of his wrist. Finished. Beth shouldn't have any complaints. Hoping she had something cold and wet in the refrigerator, he headed toward the kitchen.

He smiled at the unique color scheme—lavender walls and pale-gray cabinets. The white appliances seemed out of place until he noticed another traditional touch—ceramic molds hanging on the wall. The lady had taste and flair.

After he poured two glasses of apple juice, he carried them to the front porch. Beth's bare legs and feet were curled up under her, her head lolled against the chair-back. She looked young, innocent, vulnerable.

Her eyes were closed. Softly, he asked, "Are you sleeping?"

Her lids fluttered open. "Almost."

Her sleepy voice brought candlelight and long, slow loving to mind. Her dark-brown eyes reached to his soul. "How do you feel?"

She didn't answer him. Her gaze was glued to his chest. Her awareness made his nipples harden as his body acknowledged desire for her and tingled from his forehead to his toes, an odd sensation that left him speechless. He felt naked and at risk, but he wanted nothing more than to delve his tongue into her mouth and press his body into hers until need drove them as far as they could go . . . and farther.

When Beth raised her eyes to his, the two of them were suspended in time, hypnotized, shocked by the electricity forking between them. Nash took a step forward, but the movement broke the spell. She looked away first, flung her legs to the ground, and sat up straight.

Nash felt as if he had to explain his seminude state. "It was hot in there and I thought I could wash the paint from my skin easier than from the shirt." Her line of vision went from his face to the speckles of yellow on his skin and chest hair. When her tongue nervously slipped across her lower lip, he suppressed a groan.

She slid forward to the edge of the chair. "Is one of those for me?"

He handed a glass to her. "It sure is."

She took a few swallows. "I feel much better. No headache. I guess it was the fumes."

"You shouldn't go in yet. Not to stay. I'm on my way to Shannon's for dinner. Why don't you come along?"

Beth looked at him as if she was trying to figure something out. "I don't want to barge in on a family supper."

"You wouldn't be barging in. I know Shannon would like to meet you."

"Why?"

"Because I've mentioned you and she's curious." So curious she third-degreed him every chance she got.

"Nash, after last Saturday night I thought you'd realize—"

"That you don't want to get involved. We're not getting involved. You need something to do for the next few hours until your living room airs out. Believe me, with Shannon's kids around, you and I won't have a moment alone. You're safe for the evening."

She slid her fingers down the side of the sweating glass. "You're sure I won't be intruding?"

He could see she was tempted. "Positive." Then

something made him ask a question. "Do you like kids?"

She shrugged. "I don't know. I've never been around children much, being an only child. And most of my friends put their career first and are just now beginning to think about starting a family."

Honesty. He was learning to expect that from her. He'd known women who pretended to like children because they knew he did. "Shannon's three kids will give you a crash course in how kids drive adults crazy." He set his glass on the top porch step. "I'll go home and shower and be back in half an hour." He bent his head toward the living room. "Don't spend any more time in there than you have to."

She nodded without giving him an argument.

He smiled.

As he strode to his car, he felt like whistling.

FIVE

Nash led Beth to the backyard patio of a brick rancher. Shannon's youngest son, Davie, came running and threw his arms around his uncle's legs. The tight hug reminded Nash how much he loved the little boy. Would he ever have the precious opportunity to love and care for another child of his own?

The four-year-old broke into Nash's thoughts. "Mom said you were bringin' someone. What's her name?"

On Beth's insistence Nash had telephoned Shannon to make sure a guest wouldn't be a problem. He ruffled his nephew's hair. "Why don't you ask her?"

Davie became the epitome of shyness, releasing Nash's legs but standing merely an inch away. His forefinger went into his mouth and he looked down.

Beth didn't move closer, but crouched to his eye level. "My name's Beth. I'm a friend of your uncle's."

Davie's finger slipped out of his mouth and he eyed her carefully. He must have decided she was acceptable, because he asked, "Do you shoot marbles with Uncle Nash? I do that with my friends."

"We've never done that," she said with a quick glance at Nash.

"Then what do you do?"

Suppressing a smile, Nash interrupted. "We jog together."

Davie looked up at him as if that wasn't a satisfactory replacement. "You oughtta teach her about marbles."

"I might," Nash said seriously.

Davie grinned. "We can teach her now. I'll go get Roger." The small boy took off at a run toward the house.

Beth stood up straight and swept a few curls behind her ear. "You handled that well."

"I'm practiced. Come on." He curved his arm around her shoulders to propel her toward the back door. She felt right in his arms. That's where he wanted her to be. "Before the boys snare you, I want to introduce you to Shannon and Wayne. Since the house is air-conditioned, we're having dinner inside."

Nash was proud of his sister. She welcomed Beth and didn't ask too many questions. He watched the two women interact and they seemed to like each other. That was important to him because . . . Just because.

It was difficult to sit next to Beth at dinner and not want to touch her. When he surreptitiously helped Shannon's middle son Jason transfer cauliflower from his plate to Nash's, Beth bumped his elbow.

"You're aiding and abetting a minor."

Nash was unrepentant. "It's because he's a minor that he needs to be aided and abetted. How many adults do you know who eat cauliflower?"

She thought about it. "All the adults at this table."

"I mean adults who have a free choice. Even Shan doesn't like the stuff. She cooks it because she thinks she should."

Beth smiled.

He wanted to kiss her, but his nephew brought him back to the table. "What's for dessert?" Roger spoke as he forked the last mound of mashed potatoes on his plate into his mouth. "Mom said you bought something special at the bakery this morning."

Nash winked and licked his lips with a smack. "Black forest cake." At the boys' puzzled expressions, he elaborated. "Chocolate cake with cherries and whipped cream."

"Nash is here so often he feels he has to contribute to the food budget," Wayne explained to Beth. "He doesn't realize the weekends he gives me and Shannon the time to be alone are worth at least ten years of daily meals."

Beth inspected Nash steadily. "You baby-sit?"

Something in her expression said she liked the idea. "Nope. They aren't babies anymore. We hang out at my place. They appreciate a change of scene, too."

"And we get to appreciate the house without the wonderful voices of children," Shannon added.

Nash pointed his finger at her. "You miss them. You can't wait till they come home Sunday night."

Shannon sighed dramatically. "You know me too well."

Wayne pinched her cheek. "Not as well as I do."

She squeezed his hand lovingly.

Nash's chest tightened. He wanted that. The silent communication, the inside jokes, the ability to be so close to someone he could read her mind. His eyes rested on Beth. He wished he could read her mind.

While Nash and Wayne enjoyed second pieces of cake, Davie dragged Beth off to show her his collection of marbles. The other boys followed. When they all gathered in the living room again, the boys rough-housed with their father and Nash. Arm wrestling turned into body wrestling and tickling.

Finally Shannon interrupted the fun. "Time for bed."

After a chorus of "Aw's," Davie piped up. "Can Uncle Nash put us to bed?" He turned to Beth. "He tells great stories. I like the one about alien invaders who zap everybody with a laser so they can sing rock music."

Beth's brows disappeared under her curly brown bangs. "I'd like to hear that."

Nash looked at his nephews. "No women allowed. We guys have to have our secrets."

"It's okay," Roger claimed to Nash's surprise. "We can trust her. Anybody who can shoot a marble that far on the first try has to be okay."

A warm glow burned in Nash's heart.

Shannon smiled. "Wayne and I will set up Trivial Pursuit and start another pot of coffee."

While the boys changed into their pajamas, Beth stopped Nash in the hallway. "If my presence will bother you, I can stay in the living room."

Her presence bothered him, but not the way she meant. Her hand on his arm started his libido smoking, but he knew she wouldn't mock his efforts at storytelling or make him feel self-conscious. "You can come in. Once I get started, I'll forget you're listening. I get caught up in the story as much as the boys." He canvassed her yellow knit top and short culottes. "But I must admit, the closer you are to me, the more easily you'll distract me."

"Nash . . ." she warned.

She was close enough to touch, close enough to kiss. But he knew better than to try it here. He leaned down and put the lightest of kisses on the tip of her nose. When he raised his head, her eyes said that despite her warning, she wanted more. What was keeping her from giving in to her own needs as well as his?

From inside the room, Roger yelled, "We're ready!"

Nash opened their door. Davie slept in the single bed

on the left side of the room. The two older boys shared bunk beds. Nash parked himself at the foot of Davie's bed. "Are you sure you want to hear about the music laser?"

Three "yesses" met him in chorus.

Nash glanced at Beth. She was leaning against the doorjamb. He turned back to the boys and began. "The planet was Ratioga in the twenty-third century. Anyone could travel anywhere they wanted by merely thinking about where they wanted to go."

Beth listened to Nash weave the story, making it colorful, relevant to a child's real and fantasy worlds. She became as entranced as the boys and decided Nash Winchester couldn't possibly have done the deeds Tom Rosenthal had accused him of doing. He was a talented architect and a good man who loved his sister and her family. That was obvious.

When Nash finished the adventure, she wondered where the time had gone. They both said good night to the boys and Nash closed the door.

She smiled at him. "You missed your calling. You should have been a storyteller."

He chuckled and shook his head. "My repertoire's limited. That's their favorite one so it gets better and better. I can't spontaneously think them up."

"What did you do the first time they asked?"

He looked sheepish. "I stumbled around and made up something about a dog and a cat. As soon as I had the chance, I sat down and outlined a couple of stories I thought they'd like." Nash appeared to be far away, as if he was remembering.

"Maybe you should think about getting them published."

His expression was pensive. "I never thought about that. Maybe when I'm old and gray and have nothing else to do."

He was so vital, she couldn't imagine him old. Nor gray . . .

"Do I have whipped cream on my nose?"

She felt herself blush. "I was imagining you with gray hair."

His eyes gleamed mischievously. "What's the verdict?"

Before she could stop herself, she reached up to first one temple and then the other. "Some silver here, and there—" Her fingers stuck in the healthy texture of his hair, the sensuousness of its feel.

Nash took her hand and pressed it against his cheek. "Do you know what happens when you touch me?"

"I . . . uh . . ." Suddenly breathing was very difficult.

"Beth." Her name was a soft plea. He moved her hand to his lips and tenderly kissed the center.

Goose bumps prickled Beth all over. She took a step closer, a symbolic step. She was still afraid and still unsure. But learning to know Nash better, kissing him, suddenly seemed to be the most sensible thing in the world to do.

He must have thought so, too, because he bent his head. But when a burst of giggles erupted from inside the bedroom and they saw a pair of eyes peeking through the slightly open door, Nash grimaced, backed away, and said in a raised tone, "Good night, fellas."

His voice lowered and was meant only for Beth's ears. "I hate to say it, but this will have to wait. It seems I have a couple of rain checks to collect."

Embarrassed her invitation had been so obvious, she started down the hall.

His hand on her shoulder stopped her. "I hope you won't change your mind." After a probing look, he took her hand and walked with her to the living room.

Shannon motioned to the card table where she and

Wayne were seated on opposite sides of the yellow, red, and blue game board. "Who's in a betting mood?"

"Gambling's illegal," Wayne remarked.

"And you're too good." Nash released Beth's hand with a squeeze and a look that said he'd rather not. "The kind of details you remember, you could help the authors write the cards."

"Look who's talking," his sister muttered as she gave each player a small plastic pie.

"Singles or partners?" Wayne asked.

"Partners," Nash decided. "That will give us an equal chance.

Wayne wiggled his brows. "Men against women?"

"Sounds good," Beth agreed, wondering how long the game would last and what would happen with Nash when it was over. A thrill of excitement made her look away from him and down at the board.

Shannon rolled the die and moved her marker to the appropriate block.

Beth soon learned everyone's specialties. Hers was Art and Literature. Wayne handled Sports and Leisure. Nash was an authority on History and Geography. Shannon excelled in Science. With much good-natured humor and arguing, the four of them moved their markers around the board.

Davie interrupted the game by coming into the room with a battered and worn stuffed Mickey Mouse. He sidled up next to Nash and grinned at Beth.

"What are you doing up, young man?" Wayne asked in a stern tone.

The little boy wiped his eyes, trying to erase the vestiges of sleep. "I heard you guys laughing and talking and I got thirsty."

"The logic of a four-year-old," Shannon explained. "There's water you can reach in the bathroom."

"But I want *cold* water."

Shannon shook her head and went to the kitchen. When she brought back a small glass, Davie downed its contents, keeping his eyes on his mother. After he set the glass on the table, he asked hesitantly, "Can Beth tuck me in?"

Shannon gave him a mother's knowing look. "If she wants to. But this is the last time anyone tucks you in tonight."

The little boy had charmed Beth until all she wanted to do was pull him on her lap and cuddle him. "Sure, I'll tuck you in. And I know you'll fall right to sleep."

Davie slipped his hand into Beth's and led her to his room. When she came back and took her seat, she asked, "How do you ever say no to him? Those big brown eyes—"

"He's a miniature con artist," Shannon joked. "And I'm really going to miss him when Jason and Roger go to school and I go back to work."

Wayne leaned toward Nash conspiratorially. "I wish you could convince her guilt isn't healthy. Davie will love day-care and time to play with other kids . . . Do all women worry this much?"

Beth defended Shannon. "I can't imagine bearing a child and *not* worrying. I guess it's difficult not to be overprotective."

Shannon shot Nash a long glance. "It's very hard."

When her brother didn't acknowledge her look or respond, Beth wondered why. Wayne cut in. "Let's get this game moving. I'm ready for another piece of dessert."

Despite Beth's well-read background and Shannon's penchant for detail, they lost to the men. To Beth's surprise, there were no remarks about male superiority. Wayne and Nash gave each other high fives and went to the kitchen for cake.

Shannon sipped her coffee, watching Beth over the rim. "He likes you a lot."

"Davie?"

"No. Nash."

What could she say? "I see."

"No, you don't." Shannon hesitated for a moment but then charged ahead. "I suppose I'm being a meddling sister, but you're the first woman Nash has brought here since his divorce. That means something even if he doesn't know it."

A curious pleasure invaded Beth. "We haven't known each other long."

Shannon crossed her legs to get more comfortable. "I'm not sure that matters. There's a way a man watches a woman when he's interested."

But what was Nash interested in? A one-night stand? A fling? The project? She didn't think he was capable of blackmail, but they wanted the same contract. "Men watch lots of women."

Shannon's cup clicked as she set it on the saucer. "Would it help if I told you Nash is just as vulnerable as you are and as easily hurt?"

Shannon was hinting at pain in Nash's past. From his marriage? Beth didn't have the opportunity to answer or ask questions of her own because Nash and Wayne reentered the room.

When Nash parked his car along the curb in front of Beth's apartment, she covered her mouth with her hand to stifle a yawn. "I don't believe we stayed so late. It was midnight before I knew it. You play Trivial Pursuit like a pro." She glanced at his profile—the high cheekbones, the determined angle of his jaw. Would he kiss her in the car or wait until they reached her door?

He unfastened his seat belt and stretched, his elbow grazing her ear. "I'm a knowledgeable guy."

"How often do you play?" she asked suspiciously as her seat belt withdrew into its holder.

"Okay, I confess. About once a month. Want a rematch after you read the encyclopedia?"

She playfully punched his arm. "I'm not complaining. You and Wayne won fair and square. Didn't you? Or did you study the cards ahead of time?"

"I'm hurt you could think such a thing."

She couldn't see his face clearly in the darkness but she could hear the laughter in his voice. "Just checking."

He shifted to face her more directly. "I pride myself on honesty, Beth. I expect it from others and I give it as often as I can."

Everything she knew about Nash told her he was sincere. But what about things she didn't know? Facts he might hide even from his family. Why couldn't she get Rosenthal's accusations out of her head? "I'd like to believe that."

His hand clasped her knee. "Believe it."

A shiver scooted up Beth's thigh and ended somewhere in her stomach. Whenever he touched her, she felt like a hand grenade whose pin had been pulled. To break the silence that had fallen, she said, "I like Shannon and Wayne."

"They're great. And life's never boring with my nephews around."

She felt electrically charged by his fingers on her skin. "I'll say. I can't believe so much energy is concentrated in three boys."

"Shannon has patience to spare. I don't know where she gets it."

For the first time in her life, Beth realized she wanted to have children. Eventually. "Maybe it comes with motherhood," she suggested.

Nash removed his hand and paused before he said, "That's a nice idea."

They'd lost their connection. He sounded remote, as if he'd moved miles away. She wanted to bring him back. "Shannon and Wayne treat their kids as if they're people—not kids whose opinions don't count."

"Yep. And when I keep them, I know they need time and opportunity to let off steam."

She could feel his attention back with her. "You have as much fun roughhousing as they do."

"I guess I do. It makes up for . . ."

She didn't think he was going to finish. But after a short pause, he did.

"For the times like that I missed as a kid."

She sensed pain in him, maybe the pain that Shannon had hinted was there. "They're fortunate to have you as an uncle."

Nash slid his fingers along her cheek. "Thank you. That's nice to hear."

His touch was searing, seductive, intoxicating. She couldn't move; she couldn't speak.

When he spoke, his voice was sandy. "Let's see how your living room smells."

They ambled up the walk slowly, as if neither of them wanted the evening to end. Nash didn't hold her hand or touch her in any way. It was maddening.

He waited as she unlocked the door. She could feel his eyes on her, searching eyes that attempted to gauge her mood and feelings. What should she do? Simply say, "Yes, I want you to kiss me"? *Cool it, girl. You're good at playing it by ear. See what happens.*

Nash flipped on a double-globed foyer light that rested on a marble-topped Victorian table in the corner. Beth moved past him and lifted the covering from the sofa. The odor of paint wasn't as powerful as in the afternoon, but it was still strongly evident. When the sheet tangled in her arms, Nash took one end to help her. They folded it in silence, their eyes locking over the crease.

When they finished, Beth reached for the covering on a chair while Nash took the one from the swing. Casually, he asked, "Do you have an air conditioner in your bedroom?"

"No. These old houses have such thick walls, I usually don't need one."

His strong arms and large hands divided the sheet in half and then formed a neat square. "I'm not thinking about the heat. Which room do you sleep in?"

"The first door on the left."

Nash didn't wait for her to ask why he wanted to know. He went into the room. She tried to see it through his eyes. Pink-and-white eyelet everywhere. He'd think it was a little girl's room, not a sophisticated woman's. She bit her lip in consternation. She had to be stylish and adult all day. At night, she liked to sink into frills and pretty decorations—from the collection of porcelain dolls on her white enamel chest of drawers to the set of lacy fans arranged with pink and white silk flowers on her wall.

When Nash returned, his expression was neutral. "You can't sleep in there. Not tonight."

"Why not?"

"It smells as bad as this room does."

"But it's better now."

He was unrelenting as he sat on the arm of the sofa. "Not good enough. If you had a headache this afternoon, you'll have worse tomorrow morning. There's no air. The humidity's holding the paint. Now, if there was a door on your bedroom—"

"No doors, just arches. Damn!" She thought for a while. "It's one A.M. Too late to call anyone to ask if they'd put up an uninvited guest. I guess I'll have to put up my tent in the backyard and sleep there."

"You could come to my house. I have two extra bedrooms."

He had to be kidding! "I can't do that."

His eyes were smoky green and compelling. "Why not?"

She panicked, not being able to think of one good reason. Finally, she managed, "Because we hardly know each other."

He stretched his long arm across the back of the sofa. "I know all I need to. I'm sure you won't gather my valuables and run off with them in the dead of night."

He was joking; her heart was thudding dangerously. Sleeping under the same roof as Nash. It was madness to consider it. Her eyes narrowed. "Why are you offering?"

He cocked his head as if the answer was obvious. "Because you can't stay here. The backyard's too dangerous if you're alone, and spending money for a motel room is a waste."

"You don't have an ulterior motive?" she demanded, hoping he didn't, hoping he did, and trying to curb an impulse she might regret.

"Speak plainly, Beth. Are you asking if I'll drag you into my bedroom and have my way with you?"

He was angry, as if her lack of trust had cut him. "I know you wouldn't do that." She innately knew he respected her and wouldn't force her to do anything against her will. But if that first kiss was any indication of the sexual feeling between them . . .

"Could be you're afraid of yourself more than me," he suggested, an edge still lining his voice.

She wanted to deny it, but sometimes her impulsiveness led her into dangerous territory.

Impatiently, he ran his hand through his hair. "This isn't a major life decision. There are doors on my bedrooms and they lock—from the inside."

He was right. For heaven's sake, she was an adult, in control of her own life. She was making a mountain out of a molehill. He was offering hospitality. Why shouldn't she accept?

She smiled. "Since I don't have an air mattress and a bed sounds much more inviting than a sleeping bag, you've got a guest for the night. *If* you let me make you breakfast in the morning."

He looked pleased but annoyed, too. "You and your deals. You don't have to repay people for their kindness."

Since her problems with John and the gossip that ensued, she was careful with what she accepted. "Pops always says debts are like dead wood. They'll sink you."

"Does your dad have a list of these sayings? They're better than Ben Franklin's."

He was poking fun, but in a nice way. "They're scattered throughout my diary. Maybe that's why I remember most of them."

He stood and slowly walked toward her. "Now that's something I'd like to read."

She knew he was serious. The disturbing gleam in his eyes told her he wanted to know *everything* about her. Fear squeezed her chest. Would he be so hospitable if he knew everything? How much faith did he have in people he cared about? It scared her even more that she wanted to become one of those people.

"A diary's more sacred than the inside of a woman's closet."

Her flip reply didn't put him off. "I'm interested in your past, Beth. I'd like to know you better." He stopped a few inches away from her and waited.

Nash had given her glimpses of all areas of his life except his marriage. He'd mentioned *when* he was divorced, not *why*. But in contrast, she'd told him very little. "My life's not unusual. I wouldn't want to bore you."

The air between them fairly hummed. His tone was even. "Let me be the judge of that."

To break the sudden tension and change the subject, she checked her watch. "If we want to get any sleep tonight, it's too late to start now. It'll only take me a few minutes to pop a few things in a bag."

His brows creased in frustration, but he said patiently, "Take your time. Neither of us has to get up for work tomorrow."

After Beth went into her bedroom, Nash sighed. He was elated that the evening had gone so well and she was coming to his house for the night. But she was still sidestepping him, being so damn evasive. What could be so terrible that she wouldn't mention where she was born, where she had worked after college, why she omitted names and places from her life before she moved to Lancaster? If he didn't trust his common sense, he'd think she'd testified against a Mafia boss and had been placed in the witness protection program.

Get real. His imagination was running away with him. She'd probably been hurt by a man in the past and disclosure was too risky. He'd have to back off and make her feel safe. She was such a delight to be around—upbeat and fun. She was a natural with kids and didn't know it. How could a woman seep into his skin, his blood, his senses so quickly, before he knew what was happening?

He didn't know how. He just knew she had. When he'd walked into that bedroom . . . It was feminine enough to make a man's head reel. Mixed with the paint fumes was the lingering scent of her perfume. The ruffles on the bedspread begged to be mussed. Damn, he wanted her. And he was going to have her. Maybe not tonight, but sometime soon.

* * *

Proudly, Nash led Beth into his house. She stood on the middle floor of the split-level gazing around the living room. "I like this! The colors are so warm and comfortable."

The living room captured the Sante Fe influence. Turquoise, peach, and rust tones repeated in the oak-trimmed sofa, loveseat, and braided rug. Authentic Indian pottery and figurines accentuated the entertainment center that lined the inner wall. A woven hanging of cattails and wheat added a dramatic flair to the rough-textured plaster.

Nash lounged against the juncture of two walls, Beth's suitcase at his feet. "Since I spend most of my leisure time here, I wanted something . . . easy."

She nodded. "It's welcoming. For working or relaxing."

It was. But sometimes it was lonely, too. Beth seemed to fill the room with an elusive element that was missing when he was alone. "If I want to work, I go downstairs."

"An office?"

"*The* office. I work out of here. That's why there's such a large driveway. So clients have a place to park."

She looked astonished. "I didn't realize that. I assumed you were located in one of the black-and-glass office buildings."

How many other misconceptions did she have about him? Did they have something to do with her reticence? "Nope. This is more convenient. Would you like something to drink or eat before I show you the bedrooms?"

She gazed through the arch into the dining room and kitchen beyond. "No thanks."

He picked up her overnight bag. "Then it's time to choose a bed."

The first room he showed her had what looked like

two single beds. The red-white-and-blue striped wallpaper shouted color and life.

Beth studied the room with interest, her eyes lingering on the fire engine collection in the corner. "Shannon has three boys, but there are only two beds."

"One's a trundle. You're welcome to this room, but I think you'll like the next one better."

She followed him across the hall to a bedroom done in plum and green. "This is more my speed." Going to the bed, she reverently touched the patchwork quilt. "Beautiful. Did you buy it in one of the Amish shops?"

He could remember his mother quilting after their dad left, every night, most of the time when she wasn't working. "No. Mom sewed it. Shannon has one almost like it."

Beth scooped up the edge to get a closer look. "Your mother must've been a patient woman. I can't imagine putting that much time into handwork. The stitches are so tiny."

"I wanted to use it in my room, but I have a king-size bed." He put Beth's suitcase across the arms of a green velvet chair. "You can use the bathroom next door. I have one adjoining my room."

She looked nervous, as if she didn't know what came next. When she moistened her bottom lip, his stomach did a jig. He moved quickly toward the door. "Why don't you get ready for bed? I'll stop in before I turn in to see if you have everything you need."

Nash left the room before he was tempted not to. Being a gentleman had its drawbacks. He took his time undressing. He slept in the nude in the summer, but in deference to Beth's presence, he pulled on a pair of black flannel jogging shorts. To give her plenty of time, he used the bathroom, brushed his teeth, and pulled down the covers on his bed.

When he stopped at Beth's room, her door was closed. He knocked lightly. She opened it and his breath whooshed from his lungs. A sexy angel. Hair loose and fluffy as if it had just been brushed. Just-washed pink cheeks. A pale-blue satiny robe covering a nightgown of the same color. A tiny bow held it closed. One tug . . . In a few minutes his shorts wouldn't disguise the passion he was feeling.

The pulse at her throat was thumping rapidly as she asked, "Do you have any hangers? There aren't any in the closet."

"Hangers?" It took him a second to realize what she was asking. "Yeah. Sure. I'll check the dresser."

He slipped by her into the room, his bare chest brushing her arm. He watched her eyes turn coffee-black and he swallowed hard. Stopping at the dresser, he felt her eyes on his shoulders, down his spine. He removed a handful of hangers from the bottom drawer and laid them on top of the cherry dresser. Then he turned around. She was standing by the bed, her eyes giving off conflicting messages of fear, desire, and need.

His heart leaped in his chest. "I've wanted to kiss you all night, Beth. If I don't do it soon—"

"Do it," she whispered.

Her neck was long, creamy, the perfect territory for his lips. He nuzzled her collarbone with his nose as his hands threaded in her hair. She was trembling, and when his lips caressed the sensitive skin behind her ear, she murmured his name.

"What, baby?"

Her fingers clutched his shoulders and she pushed back. "Kiss me."

She rose on tiptoe so her lips could meet his. He had no chance to think when the tip of her tongue slipped along his lower lip. Desire stampeded through his blood as he opened his mouth over hers and probed everywhere he could reach.

He felt her knees buckling and he backed her onto the bed, coming down on top of her. The first kiss led to another and another, her mouth and tongue as greedy as his. Kissing wasn't nearly enough. Over the satin his hand slid from her knee up her thigh. Tugging open the bow with his teeth, he rubbed his chin between her breasts and tasted skin as sweet as ambrosia.

Her presence in his life created background music that made everything more alive, louder, brighter. She was sunshine and blue sky and he wanted her for himself. He needed her more than he'd ever needed anyone. He wanted to make love to her until all her barriers dropped and there was no more fear in her eyes. He could kill the bastard who'd put it there. Whatever her secret was, it was keeping her tense, keeping her from being unself-conscious in his presence. Until now. This was the real Beth—the passionate woman who gave without reserve.

When he palmed her breast, she arched into him and moaned. Her hands were climbing his shoulders, his arms. They sought to learn more. She found the long muscles of his back and stroked. He sucked in his breath. Insinuating his knee between her legs, he tugged up her gown. She stretched toward him as her hand roamed over his buttocks and began a trail toward his groin.

Her tactile exploration was driving him crazy. His arousal was so demanding that he feared much more of her taste and touch would lead him too far. He gripped his control and prayed his mind could win out over his body. If it had to.

"Beth. Baby. Do you want this as much as I do?"

SIX

Beth had been drowning in the erotic texture of Nash's muscles, the burning of his lips on her skin, the wild desire she'd never experienced before. His rumbling baritone slid over her. Yes, this was what she wanted. She had to surface to tell him. If she opened her eyes, she wouldn't need words because he could see . . .

"Beth. Tell me this is what you want."

She opened her eyes slowly. His breathing was fast and hard, there were beads of perspiration on his forehead, and she suddenly realized where her hand had been headed. She froze.

He muttered, "I thought so," and levered himself away from her, lying on his back and staring at the ceiling.

Red-hot embarrassment kept Beth immobilized. After a few minutes, she found her voice and her nerve. "Nash, I'm sorry. I didn't realize what was happening."

He stretched on his side, propped his chin in his palm, and arched his brows. "It seems to me you were an equal participant."

"I was." She felt as if she was about to put her head in the lion's mouth, but he deserved the truth. "I wanted to be. But when you kiss me, I lose all perspective and the world spins and—"

His smile began in his eyes and spread to his mouth. "I know what you mean."

Beth adjusted her nightgown and pulled the robe across her breasts. Sitting up, she tied the bow with careful deliberation.

"That's as practical as slippers in a snowstorm."

She remembered how he'd opened it, his mouth on her breast. Her heart fluttered. "It's meant to be dainty, not practical."

Nash came to a sitting position next to her and lifted her chin with his forefinger. "I want to make love to you."

Her mouth went dry and her voice cracked. "I know."

His thumb skimmed her chin. "You want it, too, but you're scared and you won't tell me why."

"I'm not sure I'm ready to let a man into my life right now."

He dropped his hand. "You've been hurt?"

In many ways. Not just by John's selfish manipulation, but by all the people, many of them who professed to be friends, who hadn't believed her. She nodded.

"You can trust me."

She felt the tenderness emanating from him and the gentleness. "I want to." To risk trusting him . . . so soon . . .

"But I have to earn it."

Maybe he did. Maybe he had to prove to her he was different, that her feelings mattered, that he'd never selfishly turn on her for his own benefit. "Give me some time, Nash."

He played with a curl on her shoulder, sending delicious shivers up her neck. "We're adults, Beth. I don't want to play games."

"No games." She just needed more time to absorb what Nash's presence could mean in her life.

Beth became self-conscious as her breasts peaked under the satin nightgown. Looking at Nash, smelling him, sitting this close with knees touching, rattled her. She knew she should hold back, wait, use common sense rather than giving in to her desire or her growing feelings for Nash. But the other part of her wanted to play in his chest hair, see him naked, feel him hard and strong inside her.

His finger trailed over the shell of her ear, down her neck, back up to the point of her chin. He brushed the rough pad of his thumb slowly over her lips. She couldn't control her quiver of response.

"I want to kiss you again. Just kiss you."

He was assuring her she didn't have to be afraid, that he wouldn't do anything she didn't choose. "I want you to kiss me."

She braced her hands on his chest when his head lowered, as if she could anchor herself for the storm about to break. His arms enfolded her. She slid her hands up to his shoulders and waited.

He didn't kiss her right away but pecked at the corner of her upper lip, the lower, rubbed and coaxed and caressed. With tiny flicks of his tongue, he slowly tasted. The kiss began slowly and sweetly but intensified until Beth's fingers tangled in Nash's hair. When she pressed closer, his tongue stabbed hers, swept to the roof of her mouth, fluttered, then slowly pulled back.

Dragging his lips from hers, he dropped his arms and so did she. "We're going to go up in flames if I don't get out of here," he said in a raspy voice. He rolled off the bed and walked to the door.

If he stayed much longer, she wouldn't want him to leave. As it was, she felt like a jumble of mismatched pieces. She followed him.

Nash nodded to the doorknob. "Like I said, it locks."

She curled her fingers around the edge of the door to give her support, to keep her on the right side of the threshold. "Thank you for everything you did today. The painting, the invitation to Shannon's, offering me a place to sleep."

He tipped an invisible cap. "Just call White Charger Limited. Always at your service." With a grin and a wink he added, "I'll collect for the paint job another time." He gently stroked her cheek. "Get some sleep. I'll see you in the morning."

As he walked down the hall, Beth closed the door. She didn't lock it. Maybe trusting again wasn't so difficult after all.

Beth had tried to sleep, but the sandman hadn't obliged. When she sat on the edge of the bed in the morning, she stared at the tangled sheets in dismay. Unbidden, flashes of Nash's bare chest and powerful legs, his moist lips, created vivid images and erotic feelings. Had Nash fared any better? Or did he possess the ability to carefully divide his life into sections, not letting one interfere with the other? Was out of sight out of mind?

She had known that type of relationship. Her first serious one. It had ended right before she met John. But John had been sympathetic, affirming, assuring her that all men weren't selfish and she'd find the right one eventually. Hah! John had only reinforced her doubts. He had come first—what *he* needed, what *he* wanted, what was easy for *him*, and to hell with *her* life.

Nash seemed different. So honest. She'd grown up

with honesty. It was her nature. She needed it in her life from the people she cared about most. An elusive hand seemed to tap her on the shoulder. *This time you're going to make sure.* It was about time her guardian angel did her job. This time Beth would set impulse aside and listen.

She dressed in an orange-and-white striped terry romper and went to look for Nash. He was nowhere to be found. When she entered the kitchen, she saw a note on the refrigerator. "Went jogging. Be back soon. Nash."

There were no crumbs on the off-white counter, no coffee perking, no pans on the coppertone stove. Beth doubted if he'd made breakfast. Snooping in the refrigerator, she found bacon and eggs. After searching in the knotty-pine cabinets, she also located pancake mix.

She was frying the last of the bacon when she heard the sliding-glass doors in the dining room open. Nash appeared in the kitchen and her heart jumped to her throat. He looked rugged, sweaty, male, hot . . . and delicious.

He flipped off his sweatband and grinned. "Smells good. I'll get a shower and be right back. If you wait to start the pancakes, I'll help."

Did he actually believe in doing his share? It would be so easy to fall head over heels in love with this man. *Guardian angel, where are you?* She responded to him quickly. "I can manage. Take your time."

Nash didn't waste any time as he showered and dressed. Beth in his kitchen drew him and filled him with . . . contentment. Unlike many bachelors, he kept his larder filled because he cooked often. But seeing Beth at the stove, the table set, the scene welcoming, stirred lost hopes and repressed yearnings.

When he returned to the kitchen, food was on the

table and Beth was pouring the last of the batter onto the griddle. "You can start before everything gets cold."

He walked up behind her. "I'll wait." He watched her flip a pancake.

"You're making me nervous."

He longed to brush her hair aside and kiss her neck, but he didn't feel that freedom or know how she'd react. She might be trying to forget last night ever happened.

"Can't have that," he replied as he crossed to the table, picked up a piece of bacon, and popped it into his mouth. "Terrific. Almost as good as when *I* make it."

Beth brought the pancakes to the table. "Your modesty's showing."

Her quip relaxed him. "Your eggs look better. Mine stay wet. Jason won't eat them."

The pancake turner stopped in midair. "You cook when they stay?"

"Even McDonald's gets old." The small talk was driving him nuts. He stepped closer to her. "About last night . . ." *Subtle, Winchester. Real subtle.*

Beth looked as if she expected bad news. "What about it?"

"I was afraid you wouldn't be here when I got back this morning."

"Why?"

Was that relief in her eyes? Had she entertained the same doubts? "You usually run away when I try to get close."

"I don't run—"

"Back off?"

She thought about it, then said softly, "I'm not backing off now."

He felt as if he'd swallowed a jigger of whiskey that

went straight to his head. "No, you're not." He circled her waist and gave her a slow, lazy kiss. When he lifted his head, the look in her eyes made him smile. It said she still couldn't believe what happened when their lips met. "I know you want to get your living room in order today, but there's an outdoor concert at the park tomorrow night. Would you like to go?"

She didn't hesitate. "That sounds like fun."

He was trying to decide whether or not to kiss her again when the phone rang. He dropped his arms and went to the wall by the refrigerator.

"Winchester here."

"Nash, it's Jack Reynolds. I've collected the information you asked for. Sorry it took so long."

Nash's eyes went to Beth as she sat at the table. "No problem." He felt a pang of guilt. At this point, if he asked Beth to see pictures of past work, she'd probably show him.

"I wanted to tell you I found more than an outline of her portfolio. I enclosed copies of newspaper clippings concerning Katherine Elizabeth Terrell."

"I don't understand."

"You will when you get the file. Do you want me to go over it now?"

Nash's curiosity was piqued, but he was more interested in learning about Beth from Beth than from Jack. "No. I'll wait."

"I'll send it tomorrow morning by Purolator. You should get it tomorrow afternoon."

"Thanks, Jack."

"No sweat. Let me know if you need anything else. See ya."

Unable to think of Beth as a Katherine, Nash wondered why she now used her middle name.

"Business?" she asked as she forked eggs onto her plate.

"Yeah."

"Anything wrong?"

"No. Why?"

"You look preoccupied."

His gaze locked to hers. "The phone call's forgotten. Now I'm preoccupied with you."

She blushed. "Nash, what will Osgood think?"

"About what?"

"Us. Seeing each other. He might not think it's professional."

Why was she worried about Osgood? Unless . . . No! She couldn't respond to his kisses like that and have her sights set on another man. "I don't see why it should matter."

"I suppose it doesn't, but he's so eccentric. I don't want to hurt my chances or yours."

"This project means that much?"

She looked him straight in the eyes. "I'm not like you. I don't have a reputation. I *need* this project to put me where I want to be."

Her vehemence shook him. Was her career more important than a relationship? He suddenly realized he was interested in more than sex, more than a temporary interlude. "And nothing's going to get in your way?"

"Not if I can help it."

What did she want more? The money? The prestige? Or was she simply career-determined the way Monica had been after Christy died? And where would that leave him? "Sometimes circumstances don't turn out the way we want."

"I know," she said quietly, but she didn't elaborate.

How long would it be until she confided in him? Nash dug into his pancakes, more curious about the packet Jack was sending than he wanted to be.

Tobias Osgood telephoned Beth at nine o'clock Monday morning. Without preamble he asked, "Are you busy tonight?"

Beth rolled her eyes. He had to be kidding. She couldn't wait to see Nash, to explore what was developing between them. "I have an engagement."

"I don't suppose you could break it?"

She'd told Nash nothing would get in her way. Was that the truth or were her feelings for him already coloring her life? Her answer proved it. "I'd rather not."

"Thursday night then."

"I'm free."

"Good. I'd like you to join me for dinner. If it's all right with you, I'll have my chef prepare something here."

She wrote in the appointment on her calender. "Does this concern the resort?"

"We'll discuss that."

Beth tapped her pen against the base of the gooseneck lamp. "Should I bring my notes?"

"My dear, just bring yourself. I'll send the limo for you. Will eight o'clock be suitable?"

Suitable for what? There was only one way to find out. "That's fine. I'll be ready." And she would be—for anything.

The package on Nash's desk snagged his attention time and time again during the long afternoon. He was disgusted with himself. Over and over he'd decided the clippings inside couldn't change his opinion about Beth or what he was feeling. So he might as well not read it. Right?

Turning off the light at his drafting board, he pushed off the stool and stood at his desk. He opened the envelope, feeling like he was opening Pandora's box. He looked at the projects outline first. Some of her designs were innovative, others traditional with a distinctive use of colors. She was talented, no doubt about that.

Next he picked up the clippings, expecting to see one of her publicity layouts. But that wasn't what he saw. After he read the Xeroxed pages, he sank into his leather chair, feeling as if a bucking bronco had shaken and tossed him far and hard. This woman wasn't Beth! She couldn't be. But the photograph in the *Leesburg Sun* didn't lie. John Winston's arms were around her and they were both dressed in bathrobes.

What further proof did he need? Headlines didn't lie, did they? They were spread across more than one paper for a week, and then three months later during the divorce trial. Nash didn't make it a habit to read the daily paper, so even if the story had been covered nationally, he'd missed it.

Some of the reporting was tabloid-like. When a politician was involved, that wasn't surprising. Nor was the depth of detail. Nash read everything twice, shaking his head, disbelieving the black-and-white print in front of him. Then, like the controlled, organized man he was, he automatically took a blank manila folder from his drawer, attached an identifying green piece of tape like he used to label the rest of his information concerning Osgood, and printed Beth's name on the folder.

In a daze, he dressed for the outdoor concert, unmindful of what he grabbed from his closet. He drove his Corvette to Beth's house with his eyes on the road, a thousand questions parading through his mind, headlines from the divorce trial, snatches from Jack's report playing in his head.

When Beth opened her door, Nash forgot the questions for a moment in favor of the pure pleasure of looking at her. Two tortoiseshell combs secured the side curls. She'd tied a red oversize shirt at her midriff, letting the tail hang over her stone-washed jeans. This was another side of Beth. She had so many facets and he liked all of them. Where did Katherine Elizabeth Terrell fit in?

"I'm ready." She stepped outside next to him and pulled the door closed. "I can't wait to get to the park. Some days being cooped up in an office drives me bonkers."

He walked beside her down the cement path. "Do you like to go horseback riding?" Damn. That had slipped out without enough forethought. One of the articles had stated she'd been seen riding with Winston on more than one occasion.

"Yes, I do. Where I'm from . . ." She stopped abruptly.

"Where are you from? You've never said." He hoped the question sounded more casual than he felt.

After a fractional hesitation, she replied, "Leesburg. We have beautiful country around there that lends itself to riding. When I was twelve, Pops put a slot in the budget for lessons. I liked trail riding the best, but Mom insisted I train and ride in the shows to learn grace and form."

"Your mom's a lady," he guessed.

"A very proper lady."

What had Beth's scandal done to her parents? Had they stood by her? How did her mother react when she discovered Beth was having an affair with a married man?

"Nash, what are you thinking about?"

He had to control his straying thoughts until he decided how he was going to handle this. He never acted rashly. He wasn't going to start now. "I was just picturing how you'd look in tight jodhpurs." That wasn't entirely a lie.

Nash tried to keep his mind from drifting as he drove. Beth's background and the taunt of her perfume made him sit longer than necessary at more than one traffic light as red turned to green. He parked in a line of cars and took a blanket from the backseat.

Although his hands itched to touch Beth, he kept his arms at his sides as they walked toward the orchestra shell perched on the edge of the lake. Nash chose a spot to the back of the area and off to the side under a tall maple. Beth helped him spread the blanket.

He sat down first, his back against the tree. Beth settled next to him, her shoulder brushing his. She pulled her legs up to her chin and wrapped her arms around them. "What do you know about Tom Rosenthal?"

He checked her expression. "Some of his work is very good."

"And some isn't?"

"Why are you asking?"

She averted her eyes and stared at the lake. "I've heard rumors."

"What rumors?" Nash didn't speak indiscriminately about his competitors. He and Rosenthal weren't friends. He didn't know why but the man seemed to have a chip on his shoulder where Nash was concerned. Maybe Rosenthal was a sore loser.

"I heard he has a drinking problem."

"He *had* a drinking problem."

Beth's head came up. "You know that for sure?"

Nash shifted against the tree trunk so it didn't poke his spine. "Everybody knows it. Tom thought he was hiding his problem. He couldn't. He ran behind schedule, was late or missed meetings, drank too many martinis at lunch. But as far as I know, he's cleaned up his act. Osgood wouldn't have selected him otherwise."

Beth looked thoughtful as she unwrapped her knees and leaned against the tree. Her mouth was a few inches from his. He was too aware of her beside him. *Make conversation to keep your mind busy.* "How are the ideas for the resort coming?"

She moved away slightly. "All right."

"Any blocks?"

"No. I have most of it worked out. My boards aren't finished and I need to check with a couple of nurseries, but I have everything worked out in my head."

Nash thought of the pile of incomplete sketches on his table. "I have stacks of notes and ideas, but I'm still having problems coming up with a unifying concept. If I keep working, it'll come."

After a few minutes, Beth straightened out her legs. "What makes you so successful?"

"You want to take lessons?" he joked.

"Maybe."

She was serious so he dropped the humor. "Hard work, perseverance, good ideas."

Her elbow slid into his arm as she turned toward him. "But why do you think you get contracts over someone else?"

He knew his client's taste, his rivals' weaknesses. "I turn in the best bids at the most reasonable costs. Experience has taught me cost effectiveness. If a client loves color, I find the brightest red flowers. But if he wants drama, I spend more money on a tiered shelving and find less expensive plants."

Her eyes combed his face, appearing to search for something. "You make it sound simple."

He felt he was being tested again and it made him angry because he wanted to know why. "I use logic, Beth, and sound business management. But luck's involved, too. I won't deny it. Being at the right place at the right time's important. You've never told me where *you* got started." He knew what the clippings had stated, but he wanted to hear it from her.

She looked nervous. "The name of the firm was Powers and Rathton."

"Did they work locally, statewide?"

She toyed with the tie of her shirt. "It's the firm that was under a wider umbrella. We stayed local."

"I remember. You were hooked up with contractors, interior decorators. Was that in Leesburg?"

"Um-hm."

Give her every opportunity to tell you. Maybe she was young, naive, didn't realize what she was doing. "Were you on your own?" Maybe she didn't even know Winston was married when she met him. How *did* she meet a senator?

"I lived with my parents to save money. I wanted to open my own office from the minute I graduated."

That was before she found a sugar daddy to set her up. Could that be the reason she stayed involved with Winston? Anything to further her career? "So you finally managed to pull the money together and move here."

She avoided his eyes. "I had to prove something to myself, prove that I could be successful on my own."

Powers and Rathton had fired her. Plain and simple. He had to admire her guts in starting over in a new place. But of course Winston was there to catch her if she fell. Was he involved in her life now? There was no evidence of her being kept. Her car was five years old, her apartment was by no means luxurious, her bedroom was strictly hers. He hoped. How could he reconcile Katherine Terrell with the Beth he knew? Maybe he should cut things off now before he got hurt.

The announcer came to the microphone on the podium, welcomed the public, and explained the classical program. A few minutes later music swelled around them. Beth tilted her head back against the tree and closed her eyes. Nash tried to still his thoughts and let the music soothe his soul as long shadows stretched into summer dusk and he sought to escape the turmoil inside.

One piece led into another. At the moment of a building crescendo, Nash looked at Beth. A tear escaped and rolled down her cheek.

"Beth? What's wrong?" Was she thinking about Winston, her life in Leesburg?

She opened her eyes and gave him a shaky smile. "It's silly. I get so involved in the music. This is one of my favorites."

There was no deception on her face or in her luminous gaze. She was a feeling woman who appreciated beauty. He'd been too distracted to let the music take him away. She hadn't. He wanted to put his arms around her and tell her he understood.

He patted his shoulder. "Come here."

She smiled. "Said the spider to the fly?"

"I don't bite. Just nibble. And I've been told I have a shoulder that makes a great pillow."

"Should I ask by whom?"

Could she be jealous? "By Davie. He's an expert. He has this habit of falling asleep after eight P.M. no matter where we are."

She laughed and angled against his chest, her head fitted into the crook of his shoulder.

"See? As comfortable as goose feathers."

"Nonallergic, too," she bantered.

Nash had overestimated his ability to hold her casually and keep himself aloof. Her glossy hair invited his chin to rest in its silkiness. The heat from her breast flattened against his chest penetrated his polo shirt. The span of her back beckoned his hand. They were in a public place. His blood pressure had no business skyrocketing.

Beth must have felt the increased tempo of his heartbeat. She raised her chin. Why did he want this woman so? Why did an empty part of him need her warmth, her laughter? He couldn't label it pure lust, not anymore. He searched her face, looking for the answer.

She attempted to sit up. "I can move away."

"No!" He hadn't meant to be so adamant. His arm closed her in so she couldn't move.

"Nash, I don't want to be a tease."

"I need to hold you." His gaze swept the grassy area. Most of the audience was collected near the orchestra. The closest blanket was a good twenty yards away; the darkening sky created an intimate space surrounding the two of them.

Beth relaxed against him, laying her hand along his throat. Her thumb stroked up and down. "I like having you hold me. It's been a long time since I felt safe."

He wanted to shield her, protect her, possess her. He wanted to be the only man in her life, in her thoughts, in her bed. His lips came down on hers hard—with no gentleness. He thrust his tongue into her mouth, determined to brand her, make her forget everything but him.

She might have been surprised by his vehemence, but her response proved she wasn't afraid. Her arms circled his neck as her tongue lunged against his. Nash scooped her onto his lap and with fumbling fingers untied the knot at her waist. His hand slid under her blouse and, without taking time to worry with the clasp, released her breasts from their soft cups.

When his fingers made contact, he knew his arousal was hard under her thigh. Her skin was velvety smooth, her breast was firm, her feel was heavenly.

He broke the kiss. "Touch me, Beth."

She brought one hand down and ran it along his jaw as the other one massaged his neck.

"More," he rasped.

She let her fingers stray slowly over his shirt from his neck, between his nipples, to his stomach. Then she drew circles and triangles to the strains of Mozart until Nash broke out in a sweat.

When he found her nipple and rolled it between his thumb and forefinger, she burrowed under his shirt. Her fingers were cool against his heated skin. As they danced on his stomach, he thought he'd explode.

"Baby, that feels so good, but I can't stand much more. We have to stop unless you want to get arrested for indecent exposure."

She buried her nose in his neck and slowly slipped her hand out from under his shirt. He could feel her heart beating with his as they both took deep breaths. Beth stayed perfectly still, and he realized why.

With a wry chuckle he said, "My physical condition's not going to change until you're off my lap."

She groaned into his neck. "We're supposed to be listening to a concert. I thought this would be safe."

He swatted her bottom. "I'm not sure anyplace would be safe with you."

She squirmed from his lap. "This is happening too fast."

He wanted her doubts gone, her barriers down. And he wanted to pretend Reynolds' report didn't exist. "I didn't hear you protesting a few minutes ago."

"Maybe I should have. Maybe we need time to cool off, time apart."

Anger tightened his throat. "Is that what you want?"

Beth tentatively touched his arm. "I need to think about us. If I'm with you, I'm afraid we'll end up in bed before I can do that."

Her hand looked fragile, delicate. "How much time?"

"I don't know. A few days. A week."

He pulled his arm away. "Fine. You've got it. Give me a call when you're finished thinking."

From the look on her face, he knew he'd hurt her. Did he want to hurt her the way the report had hurt him? He rationalized. No. He wasn't cruel. Sexual frustration was making him short-tempered. Sorting things out now would be best for both of them.

Wouldn't it?

SEVEN

Beth thought about Nash as she rode in Osgood's limousine. She missed him. He'd been cool and polite after the concert, taking her straight home. No kiss, no hug, no "I'll see you." It was up to her now. She had to either let him in or shut him out. He'd made it clear, he wouldn't stay in between. But could she trust him? Could she tell him about John? She didn't know. But she had to see him.

The more she'd thought about Osgood's invitation, the more she wanted Nash's opinion on how to handle it. Maybe the man was having a one-on-one dinner with each of them. She'd used the possibility as an excuse to call Nash at his office this afternoon. But his secretary had told her Nash was at a construction site and wouldn't be back the rest of the day.

Later, Beth had called him on his home line, but the machine answered. She'd left a message for him to call, but he hadn't by the time she'd left. So. She'd dressed for this dinner in a green silk shirtwaist, hoping it wasn't too casual or too dressy.

When she arrived at the Osgood mansion, the butler

showed her to the solarium. Osgood's Armani suit gave him a formal look.

He came toward her with a glass of red wine. "California's best. I've invested in a few vineyards. Tell me what you think."

She took the glass, smelled the wine, swirled it, and tasted it. "Wonderful bouquet, clean taste, smooth and full bodied."

"Well, well. An expert." He motioned to the rattan Empress chair and waited until she sat before he took the sofa across from her. "Where did you learn the skill?"

"My father taught me."

"Was he a connoisseur?"

She smiled. "In a way. He owns a tavern. But he taught me respect for alcohol, how to enjoy it, not abuse it."

"Well said. Respect for any pleasure will keep it from becoming a vice. Pleasure is important in our lives. Don't you agree?"

A red flag went up. *Don't dive in with both feet.* "Uh, I'm not sure exactly what you're asking."

Osgood appraised her steadily. "There's happiness and there's pleasure. We can't always find happiness, but we can always surround ourselves with things or people who please us."

His "we's" made her nervous. She didn't want to be lumped on his side of the fence. She lifted her hand to motion to the oriental carpet, Warhol painting, and Ming vase on display. "You have a lot of beautiful things to please you. I hope you have happiness, too."

He waved his hand, dismissing the notion. "Happiness is overrated. It's elusive. We could chase after it and never catch it. I believe in tangibles. What I can see, taste, smell, hear, feel."

Her voice took on a stern edge. "Money makes that possible. Less fortunate folk strive for happiness."

"And you?" he slid in easily.

"Sometimes I'm happier than others. Pleasure's a bonus that usually carries a price tag—monetary or emotional."

He rubbed his fingers across his chin pensively. "That's an interesting concept, but it depends on the person. No emotional investment, no emotional price tag."

Beth slid to the edge of her chair. "Mr. Osgood, can we stop speaking in code? I'm not sure what we're discussing."

"We're discussing reality. If you get this project, your future will take a different course. More income, more publicity, more rich clients."

"That's why I want to design the resort," she said cautiously.

"I can give it to you."

He meant now, tonight. She attempted to remain composed. "At what price?"

His eyes became probing, his tone conciliatory. "I'd rather think of it as a trade. I give you the job of your dreams, you give me your . . . presence."

Stay cool, Beth. Stay calm. Don't blow up. She felt her cheeks reddening. "Mr. Osgood, please explain 'presence' so I don't entertain the wrong ideas."

"Presence means you're by my side when I need you, whether it's at a dinner or in my bed."

The gall of the man! How could he discuss something like this as if it were a business deal? Could he be serious? She was so flabbergasted, she was speechless.

"I've taken you by surprise."

"Do you know what you're suggesting?" Her voice rose and she knew she had to get a grip on herself, but it was more important to tell him how she felt. "Do you realize I'd be selling out everything I believe in? Yes, I want this project. But I want to earn it because my ideas are good, my presentation is the best. I won't lose my self-respect to climb the career ladder.''

He was unruffled, unperturbed, unemotional. ''I didn't realize you were a feminist.''

''Whether I'm a feminist or not isn't the issue. To put it plainly, I won't sell myself to get ahead. And if that means I'm out of the running—''

He held up his hand. ''Now, now. Don't get excited. I'm not a stupid man. An egomaniac maybe, but never stupid. You're a courageous young woman who knows her own mind. You know what's good for you. I didn't get to be a millionaire by becoming bitter or vengeful every time I didn't succeed.''

She lifted her chin and stared at him squarely. ''So if I turn you down, I'm still in the running?''

''If? Is there still a possibility you'll accept?''

She shook her head vehemently. ''No, sir. I merely want to know where I stand.''

''You stand high in my regard. Your decision won't change your chances to win my contract.''

Did he know about John? Is that why he'd put forth the proposition? ''I have to ask you, Mr. Osgood. Have you heard something about me, have I said anything to make you think I'd consider your . . . proposal?''

''No. I like what I've seen of you. Surely you know you can catch a man's eye without trying.''

''I . . . uh, I've never thought about it.''

He grinned, lifted his glass for a sip of wine, and set it down again. ''That's what makes you so tempting. You don't try.'' He must have sensed her discomfiture because he said, ''I can see I'm embarrassing you.'' He leaned forward. ''Beth, you're a delight. Especially when you eat chili.''

If she could have burrowed under the parquet floor to hide, she would have. "You saw that."

"Um. I also saw Winchester's ministrations. Is he the reason you're turning me down?"

Osgood might be eccentric, but he was perceptive, too. "No. I mean, we've become friends but . . ."

His eyes twinkled knowingly. "I see."

She picked up her wine and took a healthy swallow, not knowing what to expect next.

Osgood stood and offered her his hand. "The chef's prepared a six-course dinner. Let's pleasure ourselves."

She accepted his gallant gesture and rose to her feet. "You still want me to stay?"

"Of course. One night in your company is better than none. Unless you're feeling too uncomfortable."

"Is the subject closed? You won't try to change my mind?"

"If you mean will I make unwanted advances, the answer is no. We'll enjoy dinner as business associates."

For some unknown reason, she believed him. "Then I'll stay."

Nash brought the Corvette to a stop in front of Beth's apartment. His hair was matted from being baked in a hard hat most of the afternoon. His slacks carried dust, his shirt was sweated, but he wanted to see Beth now, before the silence stretched between them too long. That had happened to him and Monica. They'd been too afraid, or too sorrow-filled, or too unyielding, to fill the vacuum between them with their thoughts and feelings.

He hadn't resolved his disappointment and surprise at Beth's background. A phone call to Jack had been unsatisfactory. His friend didn't know any more than what the clippings stated. What bothered Nash was that nowhere in the newspaper articles were there any statements, apologies, or denials from Beth or her family.

Was that because she couldn't deny it? Had she been afraid to defend herself to the press? From what he knew of Beth, it didn't make sense. She spoke her mind. Why not about this?

The most logical thing to do was ask her about it. Get the facts. Get the situation out in the open.

Nash parked behind Beth's car. He went to the door, thinking he really should go home and change.

As he knocked, an elderly lady leading a Pomeranian on a leash down the sidewalk called to him. "Beth's not home."

He hopped off the porch and approached her. "You're sure?"

"Absolutely. I live next door." She gave him a bright smile. "I've seen your car here before."

He wondered what else she'd seen. He bet she watched the comings and goings of her neighbors with alacrity. "Beth's car is here so she must have gone jogging."

"Heavens no! She created quite a stir, she did. Everybody was peeking out their windows, standing on their porches."

What had Beth done? Walked nude down the street? "I'm afraid I don't understand."

"This *huge* gray car—limousines, I think they call them, drove right down this street and stopped in front of Beth's house. This man, all dressed in black with a hat and everything, climbed out and went up to her door. Beth must've been ready 'cause she came right out. Dressed real nice, she was."

Nash's stomach tightened and he clenched his hands at his side. Osgood. She was with Osgood! Apparently she'd made her decision. Why have sex with Nash when there were bigger fish to fry? How dumb could he be? He'd believed the innocent act. Even after Reynolds' report, he'd hoped there was some explanation, some excuse. God, he felt like a first-class fool.

The dog at the woman's feet yapped. "Hush, Ginger. I'm talking to this nice young man." She turned back to Nash. "I don't suppose you know who sent the limousine, do you?"

Usually Nash had time for little old ladies. Usually a conversation with anyone wasn't a problem, but now his throat felt like it was closing, his heart was racing, his head was pounding. He wanted to strangle Osgood, Beth . . . somebody.

Even so, he had the urge to protect Beth. "I have no idea who it belongs to."

"Are you all right? You're very pale."

Pale? He felt like death inside, like all of his dreams had been destroyed. "No, I'm not all right. Must be a flu bug. Thank you for the information." He strode to his car.

"Should I tell Beth you were here?" she called after him.

"No. Believe me, I'll tell her myself."

Nash switched on the ignition and gunned the motor, wanting nothing more than to find a stretch of straight road and accelerate to ninety. His tires screeched as he pulled away from the curb.

Letting herself into her apartment, Beth leaned against the door and sighed. What a night! She'd never met anyone like Osgood, never eaten from Limoges china, never used sterling flatware before. She had to admit dinner was pleasant, his manners impeccable. But . . . when it came time to choose his architect, would he remember her rejection? Would he count it against her? She didn't need two strikes before she started.

What she did need was a pep talk. Midnight or not, she needed to talk to her parents.

She settled on the window seat in the bay window and checked her answering machine. No word from Nash. Hopefully tomorrow. She dialed the long-distance number. Her mother answered.

"Mom, it's me."

"Hi, honey. Wait till I yell for your dad so he can get on the extension. He came in about fifteen minutes ago."

There was shuffling, the sound of another receiver being lifted. "Hi, Katie. How are you?"

"Fine, Pops."

"That's why you're callin' this time of the night?"

"I missed you. I wanted to call when I knew you'd both be home."

"We miss you, too," her mother said. "It's not the same with you so far away."

Every time Beth called or visited her parents, they tried to convince her to move back home. "Don't start, Mom. I have a good life here." And now that she'd met Nash, there was even more reason to appreciate Lancaster.

"I won't start anything. But we want to see you more often. Your dad and I were talking about driving up week after next. Will that work or are you too busy?"

"She's never too busy for us," her dad cut in.

"You're welcome anytime. With this much notice, I might even be able to get the spare room cleaned up enough that you won't have to trip over boxes to get to the bed."

"Katherine Elizabeth. You still haven't unpacked?" her mother scolded.

"Mom, it's stuff I don't use and I don't have any-place—"

"Marie, leave her alone. A few stray boxes never hurt anyone."

"Just because you're the same way doesn't make it right," her mother claimed. Beth heard her exaggerated sigh. "But I guess I can't change either one of you at this late date."

Clifford Terrell ignored his wife. "Katie, darlin', don't worry about cleanin' up. We'll stay at one of those nice motels along Route 30."

"Pops—"

"Don't argue with me. You make reservations at a nice one for next Wednesday night. And think about what you want to do. We don't have to sit around yappin' all night. Maybe we can play miniature golf."

"And don't worry about cooking," her mother agreed. "We'll take you out for a nice dinner."

"Would you mind if I asked someone to come with us?" She was met by silence. "If you'd rather not . . ."

"Of course you can invite someone," her father said. "But we would like some time just with you."

"I'll take off from work early. We'll have time. Is there a special reason you're coming?"

"No," he said quickly. Too quickly. "We just want to see you face to face. This person you want us to meet. It's a man?"

"Yes, Pops."

"Good. Glad to hear it."

After a brief conversation about what was happening in Leesburg, Beth said good night. As she replaced the receiver on its hook, she wondered what was behind her parents' visit. Sure, they missed her. But something was up. She could smell it. She'd just have to wait to discover what.

The next morning a florist delivered one red rose to Beth at her office. At first she thought it might be from Nash, but instead she found a note from Osgood saying he hoped he hadn't offended her, that he'd enjoyed her company and he would be looking forward to seeing her presentation on the fifteenth. She hoped that was true and he wasn't simply being polite.

By lunchtime she'd decided the only route to take was to practice her presentation until it was perfect, making her language as descriptive and visually persuasive as possible. While she was jotting down opening ideas, her secretary informed her Nash was on the line.

Her heart beat triple time. "I'm glad you called."

"Do you have something to tell me?" His voice was impersonal, not warm like it usually was. Maybe he was calling from a site.

"I'd like to talk to you," she answered tentatively.

"And I want to talk to you. Will you be home tonight?"

"I'll make sure I am."

"I'll be there at seven-thirty."

Beth hung up. Was Nash still angry about the other night?

She gave up trying to work midafternoon. Shopping eased the nervous tension and a hot fudge sundae comforted her for the time it took her to eat it. Buying ranunculus and daffodil bulbs to plant in September, perusing the greenhouse, helped pass another hour. By seven-thirty, dressed in a crisp yellow cotton sundress, her hands were clammy.

As soon as she heard Nash's car, she went to the door and opened it. His expression was serious when he stepped inside, but he looked good enough to eat. His fawn linen slacks and off-white oxford shirt emphasized the darkness of his hair, the richness of his tan.

"Would you like something to drink?"

"No."

She sat on the sofa and waited for him to sit beside

her. But he remained standing. "Did you want to go somewhere, do something?"

"Cut the innocent act, Beth. I know where you were last night."

"How did you—?"

His face went stiff, his eyes containing enough ice to freeze the whole state. "Your neighbor saw the limo. How long did you intend to keep it from me? Or weren't you going to tell me at all? We'd just go our separate ways. You with Osgood—"

"Hold on. I don't know what you're insinuating, but I don't like your tone. What gives you the right to tell me what I can and can't do?"

"Far be it from me to tell you what to do." His stance was purely masculine, his legs spread apart, his shoulders pushed back and straight, his jaw jutting forward with outrage. "You seem to have everything planned to the T. A concert with me. A night with Osgood. Tell me something. Was the passion between us real or did I imagine it?"

"It was real."

The wall he'd built seemed impenetrable and as hard as his voice. "But it got in the way, didn't it? You didn't plan it. You couldn't manipulate it. Obviously your conscience wouldn't let you enjoy it. All that business about not being ready was a stopgap until you could get what you really wanted. I never dreamed you were that type of woman. I believed you."

She stood. "*What* kind of woman?"

His voice was low and rumbling with restrained anger. "The kind who sells herself to get what she wants."

The words ricocheted around her heart, stinging it. Her hand came back and would have connected with his cheek, but he stopped her with a grip that hurt.

"Don't get righteous with me, Beth. I know—"

She wrenched her arm away. "You know nothing. Nothing at all." The cross-examination in his eyes disappointed her. "Somehow you've added two and two to get five! You've taken circumstantial evidence and convicted me. Have you so little faith?"

"I have faith in people I know I can trust."

"Because I wouldn't make love with you, you don't trust me? What kind of gauge is that?"

"Naked bodies breed honesty. You couldn't give me that."

His censorious tone irked her. She was sick of being judged. His mind was made up. Nothing she could say would sway him—except maybe the bare facts. "I had dinner with Osgood last night."

His laugh held no humor. "Right. I didn't just fall off the turnip truck, so don't try to give me a snow job. You can tell me the truth now."

"I *am* telling you the truth, but you don't want to hear it."

"I know how Osgood operates. Wine, candlelight, hot tub. Did he offer you the sun, moon, and the stars with the contract? Because if he did, don't believe him. He's a professed bachelor. He won't give any woman a chance to get her hands on his money."

That did it! "You have no right to judge anyone! You don't know him as well as you think you do. And if you believe what you're spouting, you don't know me."

"And you do know him? After one night? Or have there been others without the limousine that were more secretive?"

He was more stubborn than her father. Maybe a little reality therapy would shake him up. "You want the truth, Nash? I'll tell you the truth. My feelings for you scared me and I wasn't sure what I wanted to do. I have no such confusion about Osgood. I don't want him with or without his contract. Yes, he invited me to dinner last night. And yes, I didn't know what to expect. So I called you. I called to ask if he'd invited you to dinner some other time. If it was another of his trademarks. I called to ask your advice."

"You didn't. My secretary didn't leave a message."

"I told her not to bother because I'd decided to try your other line. I left a message. I thought you got it when you called today."

He looked uncertain for the first time since he walked in. "Are you telling me nothing happened?"

"Something happened, all right. He propositioned me."

"I knew it."

"Oh, did you? Well, apparently you didn't know how I'd react. I told him I wanted his contract. On merit. Nothing else."

"And he accepted that?"

"Yes. Unlike you, he believed what I said. The fact that you didn't hurts, Nash. More than I can ever tell you." Tears came to her eyes and she blinked fast. She wouldn't cry in front of him. She wouldn't give him the power to hurt her that much. "I've been hurt before. I've been misused before. I don't need this again."

"Beth—"

"I don't want to talk about it. You didn't trust me. No relationship can grow without trust. You can't believe what you did about me and have feelings for me. So get out of my life and leave me alone."

He must have heard the hopelessness in her voice and the finality. He left without a word.

When the Corvette's engine was a sigh on the breeze, Beth curled up on the sofa and cried.

Nash drove until darkness fell. He took no joy in

the spectacular rose-and-lavender sunset. One thought crowded another until he realized he'd screwed everything up because he was falling in love with Beth. That knowledge made his breath lodge in his chest. He'd slept little last night. Tonight wouldn't be any better.

He didn't need to check his machine. He believed her—too late. In an agitated state last night, he'd come home, left for a six-mile run, showered, and gone to bed. Why couldn't he have given her the benefit of the doubt? There were many reasons, the uppermost being he hated to fail at anything.

He'd failed to keep his daughter safe, he'd failed to keep his marriage working, he'd failed to get that first project of Osgood's he'd gone after. He'd had too many failures and he'd sworn he wouldn't lose again. Was life making him cynical? Judgmental?

After Christy died, Monica had found someone else to love her, to comfort her, to understand her. He'd been so devastated by his grief, he hadn't read her signals. Was that why he'd reacted to strongly to Beth's association with Osgood? *Don't give yourself an excuse, Winchester, you don't deserve it.*

Nash wasn't surprised when he found himself in Shannon's driveway. He didn't climb out, but switched on the car light and dug his wallet out of his back pocket. Searching through the inside flaps, he found what he was looking for and pulled it out.

The edges around Christy's picture were bent. He stared at her and let the emotion rise in his throat. What he missed most was holding her, tickling her, cuddling her. He missed the wet kisses, sticky hands, broad smiles. The ache would never go away. He'd accepted that. It had diminished year by year. In the excitement of getting to know Beth, he'd almost forgotten about it.

Beth. He'd easily pictured her as a mother. Hell, he

didn't even know if she wanted kids. What was she feeling right now? He'd seen the awful hurt in her eyes, the pain she'd tried to hide. The thought of Beth crying tore him up.

He slipped Christy's picture into his wallet, hit the light, and climbed out of the car. He went around the back of the house to check the patio. Shannon was sitting in a lounge chair, studying the sky.

"Star gazing?"

She smiled. "You caught me."

"It's legal."

"Good. I won't try to steal one and put myself in jeopardy." She tried to see Nash's face in the shadows of the citronella torch lights. "You look beat. Rough day?"

That was an understatement. "Rough couple of days. Where's Wayne?"

She aimed her chin at the house. "Giving the kids baths. It's his turn tonight."

Nash lowered himself into the lawn chair. "Do you and Wayne fight?"

Her shoulders lifted. "We disagree. We thrash it out. We rarely yell and scream. Why?"

"I just wondered. When Monica and I were married, it was like we had an unspoken agreement—avoid conflict at all costs. If she got angry, she withdrew."

"The silent treatment?"

"Yeah. Until the issue blew over."

"And what did you do?"

"I let her alone."

"You actually solved problems that way?"

"Sometimes."

"Get real, Nash."

"The unimportant ones solved themselves. The others . . . Obviously, we didn't know how to solve them.

I swore if I ever got involved with a woman again, we'd talk everything out.''

"But?"

"But I did something stupid. I jumped to conclusions. I found out something about Beth's past.''

"Something she hasn't told you?"

"She won't now.''

"You had a fight?"

"I don't know if she ever wants to see me again.''

"She withdrew?"

"She slammed the door.''

"You've got hands. Open it again.''

"What if she locked it for good?"

"Then instead of your hands, use your mind and your heart." Shannon's tone said she had no doubts about it.

"I'm afraid she'll never confide in me now.''

"Does it matter?"

It mattered too much. He realized he was more involved than he ever expected to be. "Yes. Because I won't know she trusts me unless she does.''

"Maybe it's more important for you to trust her.''

That socked him between the eyes. Shannon was right. If he proved to Beth he had faith in her, if he stood on that no matter what, she'd have to feel his trust. "How did you get so smart?"

Shannon put her hand over her heart and said dramatically, "It's the voice of experience. All thirty-eight years of it. I'd gladly give you a few if I could.''

"Every one of them becomes you.''

Shannon reached out to her brother and took his hand. "Everything will be all right if you follow your heart.''

He squeezed her fingers. "That's a scary road.''

Shannon didn't disagree.

*   *   *

Working wasn't the answer, Beth decided, looking around her office. Papers littered every hard surface. Drawers stood open. The office looked as if it had been ransacked. She had gone from one project to another, hoping to be inspired by something so she could focus and forget about Nash. But she couldn't. She remembered his accusations, the suspicion in his eyes, the bitter disappointment in his voice. He'd brought back memories she'd rather forget.

Her first trip to the grocery store after the newspaper carried news of her and John's "affair" had been a disaster. People had stared, whispered to each other, condemned her. Some even approached her and asked how she could do such a thing to John's family. To hers. They weren't interested in facts or denials. So she'd met their hostility with silence.

Beth left the shambles of her office. When she stepped outside, the ninety-degree heat hit her like a steam blanket. Once home, she slipped into her lightest jogging outfit of pink nylon. If she couldn't work off her mood, she'd run it off. Dropping the key into her bra, she took off at a brisk pace down the tree-lined street.

One mile stretched to two. By three she felt dehydrated and knew she had to quit. She ran until she was a block from her apartment, then walked. As sweat trickled down every patch of skin, she readjusted her sweatband so the drops missed her eyes.

A half block from her porch, she saw the navy Corvette parked at her curb. Another few yards and her eyes found Nash sitting on her porch step. Now, what was she going to do?

EIGHT

Beth stopped. She scanned Nash's shoulders pushing at the blue cotton shirt, his long legs emerging from cut-offs, and her heart tried to leap from her chest.

He stood, feet planted apart, blocking the porch.

She glanced along the side of the house, considering dodging him, running around back, and locking herself inside. She didn't need more abuse.

He folded his arms across his chest and looked like a Roman gladiator, 1992 version. "I'm not leaving until we talk."

Authoritarian, dominating, sexy, handsome . . . Damn! Taking a few deep breaths, she straightened her shoulders and walked up the steps, stepping over his foot as if he weren't there. She was aware of his eyes behind his sunglasses scorching her as she fished the key out of her bra. Unfortunately, Nash was too big to ignore. And he was too strong to dismiss. He could stop her from going inside if he wanted to. Or he was probably stubborn enough to sit on her porch steps until doomsday.

She took a stab at dissuading him. "We don't have anything to talk about."

His mouth turned down as he flipped off his sunglasses and hung them on his pocket. "Maybe you don't, but I do. I'll talk. You can listen."

She tossed him what she hoped was a withering glare and unlocked the door to step inside. Not stopping to offer him a seat, she went straight to the kitchen, poured herself a glass of orange juice, and drank it down. The trembling in her limbs was from exertion, nothing else.

His gaze followed the rise of the glass, the constriction of her throat as she swallowed. "It's too hot for jogging."

She wiped her mouth with the back of her hand, not caring if the gesture was ladylike. "I needed the exercise."

"You could have had a heat stroke."

His remark had an edge; she couldn't decide if it was annoyance or anger. "That's my business. What do you care?"

"I care, Beth. I care a lot."

Damn! His voice had the same smoky quality that was there after he had kissed her. With a snort of disbelief, she rinsed out her glass. "Yeah. You care so much you'd accuse me of . . ." Blast! She'd start crying in a minute and that was unacceptable. She plunked the glass on the counter and headed for the living room. "I have to take a shower."

Nash caught her arm in a no-nonsense hold. She looked down at his hand until he let go.

Mowing his fingers through his hair, he sighed. "I'm sorry. I don't know what else to say."

She scooted her eyes away from the hard length of his thighs, his slim hips, his flat stomach. Her reaction to his physical appeal made her explode. "You didn't trust me!"

"Do you trust me?"

Something in his eyes held her still. If she trusted him, she could tell him about John. Right? No. It was more complicated than that. Especially now.

He took a step toward her and waited to see if she'd back away. She could. She felt she should. He had jumped to conclusions, he had convicted her without a trial, he'd refused to listen . . . But she didn't back away.

Nash gently placed his hands on her shoulders. "Maybe we both need to learn how to trust."

Her body quivered and he was only touching her lightly.

His hands slid to the back of her neck and cupped her head. "I'm sorry, Beth. I figured I had tunnel vision because I thought you were getting Osgood's contract unfairly. But it wasn't that. I was jealous. I do care about you. And the thought of you with Osgood made me crazy."

"Oh, Nash." Her anger evaporated and suddenly nothing was more important than having his lips on hers. She'd missed him so much. His head came down and she leaned forward to meet him.

His lips played with hers until she opened her mouth to ask for more. His groan swept into her mouth as his tongue speared into hers, stroked hungrily, then thrust in a rhythmic, intimate motion, telling her exactly what he wanted.

She swayed, stabilized, then pressed into him, wanting to feel his arousal. Apparently he wanted to feel her softness just as much. His hands slid down her back and cupped her buttocks. Stars ricocheted in her head as his hardness met the V at her thighs.

He tore his mouth from hers and scattered kisses over her face, down her neck. "I need you, baby. I want you more than I ever thought I could." His fingers took the sweatband from her hair.

Abruptly she realized she wasn't perfumed, lotioned, and powdered. She was hot, bedraggled, sweaty. "Nash. Nash, I have to get a shower."

His eyes were glazed with desire when he gazed at her. "Now?"

"I'm a mess. I . . ."

He nibbled her earlobe and whispered, "You're perfect."

"Nash—"

He looked up again and saw she was serious. "We could shower together."

She gazed at him long and hard and admitted to herself this was what she wanted. "Yes, we could."

He swept her into his arms as if he was afraid she'd change her mind and carried her into the bathroom. Setting her down in front of the shower, his eyes devoured her. The blaze in them scared her, intoxicated her, invited her to another world—a world she could share with only him. She turned away from him and leaned into the shower, turning on the spigots.

When she faced him again, he was still watching. She took the hem of her tank top between her fingers and slowly pulled it over her head. She tossed it to the floor and he stepped closer.

His index finger traced the upper edge of her bra, bringing shivers to her shoulders. "I've imagined what you look like more times than I want to count."

Boldly, she reached out and unbuttoned his shirt. "And I've imagined touching you, more times than I want to count." She pulled his shirt from the waistband and pushed it back on his shoulders. As she slid her hand down the middle of his chest, he closed his eyes.

Leaning forward, she kissed his collarbone, rubbing her cheek in the curling hair. His body responded immediately, his manhood pulling at the crotch of his shorts. He sucked in his breath and held her away. "I hope this is a cold shower. Or the anticipation will kill me.''

She grinned. "What a way to go.''

He reached around her, trapped her in his arms, and unfastened her bra. "Do you have a sadistic streak?''

As her straps fell down her arms, she shook her head. He smelled so male, his muscles were so well defined, his sexual energy penetrated every fiber of her being, igniting a bonfire of need.

Nash held one of her breasts in each hand, bent his head, and brushed his chin over their soft skin slowly, sensually, erotically. Her world swam and she finally knew the meaning of "swoon.''

"So silky," he murmured. "So perfect.''

His reverence excited her more. When he straightened, Beth shook her head to clear it. Nash peeled off the remainder of his clothes and she followed, absorbing the power of his arousal.

He winked and grinned. "It's just me.''

Her eyes flew up to his. She bit her lower lip and climbed into the shower. Nash followed her and pulled the door shut. There were no distractions, no outside noise, only the water, their naked bodies, and the few inches between them.

Beth had never found breathing to be so difficult. Nash's eyes roamed her body over and over as if he couldn't look long enough. Finally, he asked, "Would you like to have your back scrubbed?''

His vital maleness weakened her knees. "If you're doing the scrubbing." She stepped into the water and let it sluice over her hair, down her shoulders, until her skin was wet and shiny.

Nash swept his gaze from her sleek wet breasts to her lips, to her eyes, and picked up the soap.

Beth couldn't keep her hands to herself. All that

wonderful male territory to explore. She'd start at the top. The tips of her fingers stroked his lean cheek.

Her touch activated him. He folded her into his arms, his right hand clutching the bar of soap. As the water splattered against his shoulders, he kissed her long and hard and deep, his tall frame sheltering her from the pinging wet nettles. His scorching, open-mouthed kisses started her body vibrating. The sensation began in her womb and spread to her arms and legs.

Nash released her to stare all over again, as if he wanted to savor every second. She felt her wet hair drip around her face. Nash caught a droplet with his tongue, then followed a path from her cheek to her throat with playful nibbles that made her knees wobble. At the same time, he put the soap to use.

His hand slid around her breast, covering it with a sudsy film, while his other hand rolled a nipple on the pad of his thumb. She couldn't prevent a soft whimper from escaping as he gently tucked her upper lip between his teeth and tickled it with his tongue.

This was Nash. This was excitement. This was pleasure. This was love. Her heart skipped a few beats as she admitted it to herself.

He murmured in her ear. "You are so beautiful. I want to touch every inch of your skin and make love to all of you."

Make love. Did he mean it as a euphemism? Or was he in love, too? She needed to believe he was. She pressed her lower body against his desire. "I want you to make love to me."

He whispered, "Slowly. Little by little." He captured her lips again as he stroked the slippery underside of her breasts and slowly wreathed the areolas. A tremor rolled through her and she murmured against his lips. "It feels wonderful."

"*You're* wonderful. I want to make you mine, Beth. All mine."

His possessiveness thrilled her. For the moment, he was the conqueror claiming his lady. She had no urge to resist.

He soaped her back, skated his hands over her derriere and the hollow at the base of her spine. Releasing her lips, he gazed into her eyes as his hands splayed across the fullness of her hips. It was obvious he wanted to pleasure her in as many ways as he could for as long as he could. Her heart soared because he wanted to give her that gift.

His hands began a journey to the front of her thighs. She wanted to scream, *Touch me, please touch me,* but his eyes commanded her to be patient because the wait would be worthwhile.

She wriggled, longing to feel his hands where she wanted them most. He smiled. With deliberate slowness he stroked her thighs, each time coming closer to the mysterious recesses of her flaming need. He petted with feathery lightness while his strong arm held her up, supporting her against the dizzying sensations he incited.

"Nash, touch me. Please." She couldn't wait. She'd die if he didn't . . .

His hand cupped her feminine mound. With silky fingers he touched the petallike folds where she was the most sensitive. Her eyes closed. As he probed deeper, she murmured his name. He would have taken her over the crest of her escalating passion, but she didn't want that. Not yet. She wanted to be one with him when that happened.

Gathering every ounce of willpower available, she breathed deeply and moved away from his hand.

"Baby, what's wrong? Have you changed your mind?" His voice was thick with passion and his own need.

"Nothing's wrong." She took the soap from his hand and tried to steady her breathing. "It's your turn."

While the water trickled down his chest, Beth kissed his lips, his neck. She lathered his chest, mapped his initial, then let the water rinse the dark curly tendrils before she tugged one of his nipples gently between her teeth. He released a sound deep in his throat as she sucked more firmly and nuzzled him with her lips. When she stood back, his eyes were closed. She smiled, soaped her hands, then glided her fingers over his firm stomach and forayed lower and lower. His muscles strained and tensed as he strove for control.

She whispered. "Turnabout is fair play. Isn't this fun?"

When his eyes opened they were a fierce green. "Fun? If you do much more—"

She took him in her soapy hands and he gasped. Sweet torture wracked his face. "You keep that up and I'll take you right here."

"That would be interesting," she breathed, as aroused as he was. She coaxed, provoked, and fondled until Nash grabbed her by the shoulders with shaking hands and pulled her tight against him. He tightened his hold and ground against her, pushing up into her softness. "I need you. Do you want to go—"

"Now, Nash. I want you inside me now." She dropped the soap and looped her arms around his neck. When her lips touched his, her tongue rimmed his lower lip. He tilted her hips up, lifting her until he entered her snugness and she wrapped her legs around him. A low growl rumbled in his throat as he pressed her back against the wall so they had a bulwark against the erotic waves threatening to drown them. They found their rhythm, their bodies meshing, enacting a mating ritual centuries old. As Nash thrust, Beth tightened around him and moaned aloud her sense of fulfillment. They flowed into each other, man to woman, lover to lover.

Nash was deep within, probing, questing for the trigger to unleash the wonder for Beth. She shifted toward him feverishly. "That's it!"

He stroked again and again, the driving cadence gaining speed and momentum. The universe exploded, shards of brilliant stars flashing against black velvet desire until Beth became a radiant sun, bursting into another time and dimension with an excited cry of release and awe.

She clung to him as he shuddered again and again a few moments later. She was exhausted, replete, spent. As he lowered her carefully to the floor, water sloshed around her feet, bringing her back to reality.

Nash held Beth's face between his hands and stared into her eyes. "I have never, never experienced anything like that before. I want you to know how special that was for me."

Her lower lip trembled. "Me, too."

She looked down at her toes and tried to tuck her chin down, but he wouldn't let her.

"Beth?"

She met his eyes. "I'm embarrassed. I've never reacted like that. I guess it scared me. I don't know that part of myself."

Nash drew her gently into his arms. "You're a passionate woman. That's nothing to be ashamed of."

She leaned back and saw approval in his eyes and . . . a question. He didn't ask it.

Instead, he said, "We could be more traditional and try the bed."

He wanted her again. No man had ever made her feel so special or cherished. "Think we'll be as good together on dry land?"

"Better." His voice held no doubts.

*   *   *

Nash watched Beth as she dozed on his shoulder. She was so passionate and free. Her outgoing nature was more of a turn-on than pink silk. So was the challenge that flashed in her eyes, the softness of her touch, the smile that was easy and intriguing at the same time. He'd never known a woman like her. And he'd almost pushed her away.

Fear clutched his heart. He couldn't lose her now that he'd found her. He'd lost too many people in his lifetime. He didn't know where he and Beth were headed yet, but he knew they were headed there together if he had anything to say about it.

Trust. It was such a fragile thing. They had to build it up. How long would it be until Beth trusted him enough to tell him about John Winston?

Nash was angry with himself because it mattered. He wanted to know the whole story, what Winston had meant to her, if he meant anything to her now. Was he jealous? Hell, yes. Especially after the way she'd made love to him. He wanted to know all of her and he didn't feel he did.

He smiled when he remembered Beth's embarrassment in the shower. It had been endearing. What did it mean? That she and Winston had had an ordinary sex life? Nothing spectacular? He couldn't imagine making love to Beth not being spectacular.

He still couldn't picture her having an affair with a married man. Picture it? Blazes, he wouldn't do that. But the whole situation didn't sit right. Beth was an honest woman. And open. Of course, people changed when they were in love. Maybe she'd been blind.

Don't torture yourself with this. Wait for her to trust you. Then a terrible thought entered his head. What if she discovered he'd inadvertently dug into her past? What would that do to her ability to trust?

Beth stirred next to him, opened her eyes, and smiled. "Hi."

He tweaked her nose and searched her face for what she was feeling. "Hi, yourself."

She tenderly traced her finger along his jaw. "You look so serious."

He needed an answer before his heart could be as satisfied as his body. "How do you feel?"

"Hot. I need an air conditioner."

"Beth—"

In her usual forthright manner, she cut straight to the chase. "What do you want to know?"

That was a loaded question. "Do you have any regrets?"

Her brows furrowed. "No." She squirmed as if uncomfortable with more than the heat. "Except . . . I wasn't protected. It's my safe time, but—"

He'd been so caught up in his need for her, he'd never given it a thought. "That was stupid and irresponsible. I'm sorry."

She moved away and sat up against the headboard. "It's as much my fault as yours. We both got . . . carried away."

Nash pushed himself up next to her. He wasn't going to let her withdraw. "How would you feel if you became pregnant?"

She looked him straight in the eye. "It's not in my immediate plans. Pregnancy would throw a terrific wrench into my life."

His stomach clenched.

Until she continued. "But seeing Shannon with her kids . . ." Her voice trailed off. "I would hope I could love the baby as much as Mom and Dad loved me."

She would have the child, cherish it, and be a wonderful mother. He knew it in his soul.

"How would *you* feel?" Her look was probing.

He shifted toward her and was distracted by the dampness between her breasts. "I wouldn't leave you stranded. And I'd want to be a father in more than name." This conversation was getting much too serious, especially when he'd rather be touching her again. He dragged his finger around her breast. "I'm tempted to get carried away again. Why don't we get dressed, stop at a drugstore, and go to my place?"

She pretended to think about it, to hide the gold flickers of desire in her eyes. "The air-conditioning *would* be nice."

His fingers went to her ribs. "Air-conditioning?"

"Don't tickle me," she yelped as she brought her knees to her chin to protect herself. "I hate it."

He stopped, but kept his hand on her waist. "I'd rather do something you like."

"Then we'd better hurry to the drugstore," she quipped with a saucy smile.

Nash laughed out loud, then kissed her thoroughly.

He dressed while Beth took another quick shower. She'd insisted on washing her hair even though he didn't think it was necessary. But he knew how Shannon felt about looking good, so he didn't argue.

Before he could try Beth's swing chair, he heard the clank of the mailbox. He went to the porch and fetched the cluster of letters. As he laid them on her coffee table, an embossed off-white envelope caught his eyes. He read the return address. John H. Winston. It was a Virginia address.

They were still connected in some way. How?

The sun was barely peeking over the horizon as the letter burned a hole in Beth's pocket. She peered out Shannon's kitchen window. Nash, Wayne, and the boys were playing football. Shannon was sitting in a chaise lounge watching. On the pretense of getting a drink of water, Beth had come into the kitchen.

The afternoon had been wonderful. Nash's lovemaking skills rivaled his architectural ones. Ready or not, she was in love. Was he?

He'd apologized again for his doubts about Osgood, and she realized how the situation must have looked. But if he'd jumped to those conclusions so easily would he ever believe her about John? That would really test his faith in her, and what they had was too fragile to be tested . . . yet.

Slipping the envelope out of her pocket, Beth tore it open.

Dear Katie,

I received your final payment, hoping there would be a note. Of course there wasn't. I keep looking for a sign that someday you can forgive me. Believe it or not, I did cherish our friendship and I miss it more than you could ever know.

Would you consider meeting with me? I've never apologized in person and I feel I owe you that. I've bought a farm in Virginia and am now making that my home and practicing general law. It's what I've wanted to do for years. Thanks to your silence, I'm now a free man.

I'd be glad to see you on neutral territory, at your parents' home if they'll allow it. Whatever you want, Katie.

I'll be waiting for your answer.

John

Beth folded the letter, replaced it in the envelope, and stuffed it in her pocket. She didn't want to see John. She never wanted to see John again. Betrayal was too hard to forgive, let alone forget.

Suddenly Beth heard something other than the joyful squeals of play outside. A shout, a yell, chatter. When she looked out the window, she saw everyone gathered around a prone Nash. His knee. Forgetting the letter and John Winston, she ran outside.

Shannon knelt next to Nash. Beth fell to her knees on the other side. "Is it locked again?"

Sweat stood on his forehead; his face was drawn from the pain. "It went back into place."

She looked at the mouth that usually brought to mind heat and excitement. Now she stared at its grim tightness and wanted to cry. "But it still hurts like hell?"

His shoulders jerked quickly, restlessly, as if trying to shrug off the pain. "It'll be okay. Just give me a minute."

Beth exchanged a look with Shannon. "I think you should go to the emergency room."

"The hospital?" Roger exclaimed. "Uncle Nash, you don't want to go there."

"Roger fell out of the tree last year and broke his arm," Wayne explained to Beth. "Needles and nurses don't impress him."

"Me, either," Nash muttered with a baleful glare. "Wayne, help me up. It'll ease up in a couple of minutes."

Beth and Shannon stood while Wayne lifted his brother-in-law. As soon as Nash tried to put weight on the leg, he almost collapsed.

"That does it. We're going to the emergency room." Beth's voice brooked no argument.

Pushing Wayne away, Nash balanced on one leg. "See? I'm fine."

"Take a step," Beth ordered, her hands on her hips, her mouth pursed.

Shannon's brows lifted. Wayne looked amused.

Nash tentatively put his foot down, grimaced, and

shifted his weight again. "Okay. We'll go to the ER. Aspirin isn't going to do it this time."

Beth's attitude softened immediately. He must be seriously hurting to capitulate that easily. Instinct led her rather than her common sense. In this condition Nash would want as few people around as possible.

"Do you trust me to drive your car?"

He didn't hesitate but pulled his keys out of his pocket and tossed them to her.

Wayne looked surprised. "I'll help you to the car. Beth, are you sure you can handle him?"

She grinned. "No. But if he doesn't behave, I'll call you."

Nash threw her a look that said: "I'll get even with you later."

The Corvette drove like a dream, but Beth was more concerned with the man beside her. She already knew he was a stoic in many ways. She wondered if that had cost him his marriage. If she asked him, would he tell her?

When she pulled up in front of the emergency room, she said, "I'll help you in, then park—"

He released the door handle. "Stay put. I'll manage."

"Nash . . ."

"Don't treat me like an invalid, Beth. I'm fine," he snapped and pushed the door open.

Okay. She'd let him have his way. For now.

Nash managed to climb out of the car and hop inside while Beth parked. She locked the car and hurried into the ER. Fortunately, it wasn't busy. After Nash filled out the proper forms, the nurse showed them to an examination room.

Nash sat on the table, his legs stretched out in front of him, a frown on his face. "You don't have to stay in here. There's a TV in the waiting lounge."

She dropped into an orange vinyl chair. This time

she could be as pigheaded as he could. "I want to hear what the doctor says to make sure you follow orders."

He dragged his hand through his hair. "I run my own life, Beth. I don't need—"

"Someone to care about you?"

He appeared sorry he'd said anything but muttered, "I don't like to depend on anyone."

"Is that why your marriage didn't work?"

Lines of anger creased his brow for a moment, then eased away. "Maybe. I felt I had to keep a lid on my feelings."

How much could she probe without probing too far? "Your wife couldn't accept them?"

He seemed hesitant but not closed. His eyes narrowed as he remembered. "I didn't give her the chance. Monica was . . . reserved. She didn't ask questions. I didn't give answers. Maybe if I hadn't spent so much energy on my career . . ."

Beth waited a moment before she spoke. "It doesn't sound like you were friends."

He shifted on the table and winced. Instead of taking her lead to talk about his marriage, he asked, "Are *we* friends?"

"We're working on it." Sensing his reluctance to review the past, she moved away from the topic. "You know the real reason I came back here with you?"

"Why?"

She smiled and whispered, "To see how sexy you'd look in a drafty hospital gown."

His cheeks flushed.

She poked him in the arm. "Are you blushing?"

"Of course not." He chuckled wryly. "Maybe. I'm not used to a woman being so—"

"Forward?"

His eyes caught hers, held, caressed. "Openly complimentary."

Hadn't he been involved with anyone since his divorce? If not, why not? He was sexier than any man she'd ever met. Even in a hospital gown. A fantasy began to take shape.

The doctor entered the cubicle, cutting off Beth's hot thoughts.

Beth opened the door to Nash's house and waited as he maneuvered inside on his crutches. He swore when one caught on the edge of the rug.

"You'll get used to them." She smiled encouragingly.

He sent her a dark look and readjusted his stance. "I don't have to get used to them. I only need them for a few days."

She stared at his taped knee as she laid her purse on a chair. "Right now you need to get the leg up." At his scowl, she realized what she'd said and how she'd said it. "I'm sorry. I'm not trying to tell you what to do."

The scowl transformed into a sly smile. "Aren't you?"

She felt her cheeks grow hot. "Do you want a pain pill?"

He glanced at the bag she held in her hand. "The knee's pretty ragged. But I hate the way they make me feel."

"Like you're depending on something artificial?"

"Exactly. But I could be persuaded to take one if you come lie with me. We can watch television in bed."

He looked dead on his feet. Resting beside him wouldn't be a hardship. "Go get comfortable. I'll bring in the pill with a glass of water." She knew if she offered to help, he'd refuse.

Fifteen minutes later, Beth went into Nash's bedroom balancing a tray holding two glasses of iced tea and a dish laden with crackers and cheese. Nash's chest was bare, the sheet pulled to his waist. Her stomach jumped as she wondered if he was naked.

His face lost some of its tired quality as he saw the food. "Great. Supper was a long time ago." The smile dissipated. "But don't feel you have to wait on me."

She handed him a glass and the pill, wanting to smooth his hair from his brow. She'd never realized she had such a strong nurturing streak. But she had to put it in terms he'd accept. "Remember when you painted my living room, then brought me something to drink?"

Nash threw the pill in his mouth, took a few swallows—and nodded.

"I'm returning the favor." Her fingers went to her blouse buttons and unfastened them.

Nash's eyes followed her movements. "I called Shannon so she wouldn't worry. Told her I just had to take it easy for a few days."

Beth wondered where her need for Nash came from. She'd never experienced anything like it before. It seemed bottomless, encompassing. Her heart beat faster. She shed her blouse and laid it on the Windsor rocker. "Good."

Nash licked his lower lip as she unbuttoned her shorts and stepped out of them. Beth saw the passion come alive in his eyes and suddenly realized she was unwittingly performing a striptease. Not a bad idea. It would take his mind off the pain until the medicine worked. Her movements became more seductively calculating and she decided his discomfort wasn't her only motivation. She felt powerful turning him on.

When she reached to her back to unhook her bra, she did it slowly. Her breasts thrust forward.

Nash groaned. "Do you know what you're doing?"

Her thumbs went to the panties and rimmed the waistband back and forth, back and forth. "Um-hm."

His voice was husky. "You're a tease, Beth Terrell. If I could, I'd do something about it."

She was all innocence as she slid the panties down her legs with a gentle sway of her hips. "Why can't you?"

"Because I can't move the damn leg!" he growled.

She lighted on the bed, one leg up, one leg down in a centerfold pose. "If you're really interested, you wouldn't have to move your leg. But I guess you'd have to sort of . . . depend on me."

Nash's eyes darkened. "You're full of surprises."

She couldn't tell if he approved or not. Maybe she'd read him wrong and she was turning him off, not on. Only one way to know. "Is that good or bad?" She held her breath and waited for his answer.

NINE

Nash's grin split his face as his green eyes dazzled her. "*Very* good." He threw back the sheet and crooked his finger at her. "Come here."

Her stomach muscles tightened at his sexy tone. But when she crawled into bed and the mattress sagged, she saw him wince. He was disguising the amount of pain he was in. It was time to show him he didn't have to perform to please her.

Reaching to the nightstand, she picked up the remote control and switched on the TV.

"What are you doing?"

Slowly, she sidled up next to him. "Going back to plan A."

His eyes became shadowed. "If you don't think I'm capable of—"

She tenderly brushed his hair from his forehead. "I know how capable you are. Remember me? I've been in this bed with you a good portion of today. But there's something else we can do in bed, too."

He looked at her suspiciously. "What?"

Snuggling up next to him, she laid her head on his

shoulder. "We can cuddle. You don't have to prove anything to me, Nash. I just want to be with you." She tilted her head to see the expression on his face.

"I want to make love to you." He sighed and smiled. "But holding you sounds awfully good right now."

Unable to resist, she kissed his shoulder and brushed her hand across his chest. "Rest and let the medicine work."

It wasn't long before Beth realized Nash's eyes were closed and he was sleeping. Somehow she had to persuade him to let his guard down with her. When she yawned, she pressed the remote and turned off the television. She couldn't resist running her hand over Nash's flat stomach. Her last conscious thought was how much she enjoyed touching him.

In the early hours of the morning, Nash turned his head and realized that his chin was brushing Beth's hair. He breathed deeply. She smelled so good. And it felt so good waking up with her there. He'd been lonely, isolated, restless without knowing why. She'd changed all that. He felt whole again.

He slid his fingers down her arm, relishing the softness, the beauty, the wonder of being this close to another person.

Beth turned her head and her lips touched Nash's shoulder. "How do you feel?"

Electrified. He wanted her. "I didn't know you were awake."

She smiled. "I'm not. How do you feel?"

He reached for the edge of the sheet tangled at his feet and repositioned his leg. "A little woozy. The sharp pain's gone."

"But it's sore?"

Nash slid his arm around her shoulders so he could hold her. "You worry too much."

His lips caught hers and molded her mouth. His tongue dashed between her teeth and navigated a course that was seductive and thoroughly arousing. Beth filled herself with his taste. Spicy-sweet. Male. Nash. Pressing pliantly against him, she molded her body to his like soft clay, nudging her tongue into his and stroking liberally until she was dizzy.

The pure touch of his skin against hers heightened all her senses. She inhaled his masculine scent, gloried in the downy texture of his chest hair. Beth was overwhelmed by her own desire and blooming love. It scared her. What would happen if Nash walked away? What would happen if she won Osgood's contract and he didn't? What would happen if he found out about John and didn't believe her?

Nash chased the questions away by breaking the kiss and nibbling her neck. She nipped lightly at his ear. Her tongue teased around the edge as he stroked her hair. Beth's pulse raced and her breasts ached for Nash's touch. She rubbed them against him to fulfill some of her need and to whet his.

His passion surged against her thigh. When he tried to roll toward her, she knew it was time to take over. With a serene smile, she pushed his shoulder down. "Lie still and enjoy."

His chest rose and fell quickly. His expression was pained. She didn't know if it was from frustration or actual discomfort. She smoothed his ruffled hair with her fingers and teasingly brushed her lips across his. When he would have grasped her tightly against him, she positioned herself lower and kissed a trail down his chest. Her hand tarried on his thigh, then voyaged up his leg. While her lips punctuated his taut stomach with kisses, her hand moved to more sensitive territory.

Nash thought he was in heaven. What Beth was doing to him defied all words. Her hot, soft lips were tasting him, her feathery fingers were stroking, toying, creating a fire he had to quench. His temperature rose as his pulse throbbed in his ears. He tried to watch her, but the pure pleasure she was giving him made him close his eyes so she couldn't see his need. Never in his most vivid dreams had he imagined her like this. He had never made love with a woman who was free enough to take the initiative. It was incredibly exciting!

Her feel and touch and texture and fragrance were driving him insane. She was pushing him to the edge of a monumental cliff and he knew he'd soon fly over the precipice.

A tremor coursed through him. He needed her. "Beth."

She lifted her head and gazed into his eyes. She seemed to know he'd reached his limit. Reaching to the nightstand, she tore open a foil packet. In a graceful movement, she straddled his legs.

Beth's naked breasts glowing ripe above him made him quake with expectancy. He felt vulnerable. As she prepared him, he thought he'd lose control. She led him inside her femininity and he groaned with the sensation. She was hot, enveloping, slick, and he fit snugly as if he'd been fashioned only for her.

He whispered. "I can't hold back."

Her eyes were huge luminous brown pools. "You don't have to. I'm as ready as you are."

His voice was thick with arousal. "No one has ever made love to me like this."

She smiled.

Beth let Nash gauge the tempo as they shimmered with the sheen of loving. Her hands quested across his damp shoulders as he blessed her breasts with erotic caresses. He tried to drive to her core, to give her all of him. His thrusting and her rocking harmonized into a steady rhythm that beat, thudded, and roared through his blood. He was lost in Beth and he didn't care if he ever found his way back.

When he soared to the highest plane, he dynamited into her, shuddering not only from the physical release but from the depth of feeling. Her intense cry told him she, too, had arrived at the same brilliant journey's end.

She collapsed on his chest. Nash held her close and knew he'd fallen deeply in love.

After the fast-beating excitement gave way to languorous repletion and Beth moved to his side, Nash reached for the sheet and settled it over both of them. Looking at her still-flushed face, the damp tendrils of hair on her temple, he didn't think she'd ever looked more beautiful.

She drew a circle on his chest. "Are you going to do what the doctor advised?"

The idea of Beth caring about him made him feel good. "Yes, I'm going to cut out the jogging and walk and swim like he suggested. Then again, there's the form of exercise we just participated in. You can be a big help with that."

She raised herself up to stare at him intently. "You're really going to listen?"

He wasn't as stubborn, arrogant, or macho as she must think. "Baby, I don't want to end up with a cane. I'll listen."

She sealed her lips to his and rewarded him.

Instead of continuing the kiss until their bodies joined again, Nash broke it off. "Will you go to the shore with me next weekend? For the past few years, I've rented a house at Stone Harbor for a week as a birthday present for Shannon. Wayne accepts it that way and gets to enjoy it, too. I go down for Labor Day weekend and join them."

She rubbed her cheek against his shoulder. "They won't mind me coming?"

He loved the physical familiarity that had sprung up between them. "They like you."

"Do you mind if I take work along? I have polishing to do on the Osgood presentation."

"No problem." Nash caressed her hip and bent his head to kiss her in earnest.

But she braced her hands on his chest. "Nash? What happens if I win the contract?" The expression on his face must have shown his surprise because she moved away from him. "You don't think I *can* win the contract, do you?"

"Now, Beth—"

Her eyes shot defiant sparks. "Don't patronize me. Do you think I can get that contract or not?"

He'd try logic to settle her down. "You haven't had much experience with commercial development."

"So?" She tilted her head and waited.

"So . . . it's more complicated . . . grander."

"And you've done so many like it, you can do it in your sleep. Don't you think maybe your ideas could get old because of that and mine might be fresher?"

He thought he knew what Osgood wanted. His concept was fanciful enough to appeal to Osgood's eccentric nature but practical enough to be well executed. He had all the confidence in the world in his ideas. Beth's portfolio, on the other hand, was limited. But if she could top his work, she deserved the contract.

"If your ideas are fresher, your presentation more eloquent, you deserve the job."

She looked taken aback. "You mean that?"

"I mean it."

"And it won't affect us?" she asked warily, searching his face for feelings he might be hiding.

"If I lose, I'll be disappointed, maybe crabby for a few hours. But I won't have lost anything."

"How can you say that?"

His voice softened. "Because of Osgood, I met you."

When she put her arms around him and sinuously moved against him, he wondered how she'd react if *he* won the job.

Saturday afternoon, Beth almost purred as Nash's large hands rubbed suntan lotion on her back with deliciously erotic strokes. When his fingers dipped dangerously close to her breast, making it peak in anticipation, she looked over her shoulder.

He grinned and shrugged, whispering in her ear, "If Shannon wasn't here, we could have some real fun."

"Is that all you think about?" she whispered back.

"When we sleep in separate rooms, it is."

They had arrived at the beach house in Stone Harbor late Friday evening. For his nephews' sake, Nash had felt it was best for him and Beth to sleep in separate rooms. "It was your idea," she reminded him.

"Yeah, and a bad one. Tonight I sneak in."

Although Nash was acting playful and bantering with her, he seemed preoccupied. His gaze kept slipping away from her and their conversation to the ocean. Maybe his knee was acting up. "What about tomorrow morning? The boys were all over you at seven A.M. today."

"I'll set the alarm," he growled as he gave her his full attention for the moment and placed a hot, wet kiss on the back of her neck. It mingled with the sensations of sand and sun and lotion.

Beth forgot where she was until Shannon looked up from the magazine she was reading and asked Nash, "How's the knee?"

"Much better. Just a little stiff. The water will be good for it." He settled himself on the blanket, stretched on his side. "Are you excited about starting work Tuesday?"

"And scared. I have to get Roger and Jason ready for school and drop Davie off at day-care before I start. I might be worn out before I begin."

"You'll do fine." Nash looked to the white-tipped waves crashing on the shore. All of a sudden, he sprang to his feet. "Where's Jason?"

Shannon's gaze followed his across the beach. "He's with Wayne. I'm sure—"

"I saw him go down under a wave." Nash took off at a lopsided jog.

Beth and Shannon hopped up, too, but before they took two steps, they saw Wayne swinging Jason out of the water. Nash was at the water's edge. He picked up the boy and hugged him.

"He must have gotten knocked over by a wave and Wayne had to help him up. I bet Nash almost had heart failure," Shannon murmured. "I never should have suggested we all go swimming. His panic is my fault."

Beth watched as Nash put Jason down and started walking down the beach as if demons were chasing him.

Surprised and confused, Beth said to Shannon, "I know he worries about the kids, but—"

Shannon darted a glance at her, not saying a word.

"Shannon, what's going on?"

Nash's sister avoided Beth's eyes. "Nothing. Just a scare."

"There's more to it than that. Why is Nash walking the beach as if he's running from something?"

Shannon's gaze followed Nash, then swerved back to Beth. "I was hoping he'd told you. He had a daughter. Christy. She drowned in their backyard pool."

"Oh, my God!" Beth started to take off after Nash, but Shannon gripped her arm.

"You'd better wait. He likes to work his problems out on his own."

With difficulty Beth deferred to Shannon. She knew her brother well. "How did it happen?"

Shannon stared at Beth for a moment. "I think Nash should tell you himself."

"I can't believe he hasn't." Her dismay must have sounded in her voice.

Shannon touched her hand. "It still hurts him. He doesn't talk about it."

"We've gotten so close." But not close enough for him to tell her about his daughter. And not close enough for her to tell him about her past. She wanted to make an excuse and say losing a daughter was different from the scandal she'd left behind. She could put her experience in the past, but Nash's would be with him forever.

She had to be alone to think. "If you don't mind, I'm going in and work for a while."

Shannon nodded sympathetically. "Nash said you might. Important project."

"Sure is. It could make me financially secure for the first time in three years. If there's any time to be a perfectionist, it's now. Call me when you need help for supper."

"Hot dogs on the beach don't take a lot of work."

Beth picked up her beach bag. "Call me anyway. When I get involved, I lose all sense of time and place."

Shannon grinned. "Gotcha."

The library table in Beth's bedroom was perfect for spreading out her sketches, markers, and pencils. But it was a while until she could put aside Nash's panic and what Shannon had told her. Finally, she concentrated with a vengeance. When her eyes began to blur, she spoke into the tape recorder, using her notes to outline her speech, then going back a second and third time to fill in. Feeling she needed perspective before she listened to it again, she went downstairs to the kitchen for a can of soda.

On the deck, Shannon sat in front of Wayne on a lounge chair, her head on his chest. The boys were building a giant sand castle. Beth smiled. She didn't want to disturb them.

Where was Nash? Still walking the beach, immersed in the past?

She popped the lid off the soda and took a few sips. Seeing a bag of pretzels on the table, she sat down and munched on one, trying to clear her head. How should she approach Nash about his daughter? Should she ask him? Would he bring up the subject?

She finished the soda, went into the living room and up the stairs. As she walked down the hall, she heard movement in her room.

She hurried, then came to a full stop as she saw Nash, his hand on her tape recorder, his eyes sweeping over her boards. "What are you doing?"

He looked startled, but recovered quickly. "Looking for you."

Her eyes went to her drawings, then back to him. An unconscionable suspicion raised its head. "Checking out the competition?"

He evaluated her question, but didn't rise to the accusation in it. "Not intentionally. There was no evidence you were coming back, so I came over to turn the light off."

She wanted to believe him. Why shouldn't she believe him? He had never lied to her. Right? But a small voice said: *He didn't tell you about Christy.* What else was he hiding? Guilt hit her again because she kept a secret, too.

Crossing to the table, she shuffled the boards into an

even pile and deposited them into the open leather port-folio on the bed. She zipped it.

"All finished?" Nash stood at the foot of the bed.

"Almost." He looked weary, the lines around his eyes deeper than usual. She nodded to the tape recorder. "I'm working on the spiel."

"You're putting everything into this, aren't you?"

"Aren't *you*?"

He shrugged. "It's one project, Beth. I can't put all my apples in one basket."

He was being awfully casual. "So it doesn't matter if you get it?"

"Of course it matters. It's an important project, a lucrative one. But I'll survive without it and do quite well."

Since when did the resort lose its allure for him? Since when did she question his sincerity? Rosenthal's doubts must have lain dormant until now. A swift ache sped through her. Had John's betrayal done this to her? Made her distrust the man she loved?

She took a step toward him. "I didn't hear you come in the house."

"We must have just missed each other."

Was he trying to convince her he wasn't in the room long? "I was in the kitchen. Have you been walking all this time?"

"No. I'm not pushing my luck. The knee feels good."

Should she bring up Christy now to see how he'd react? She couldn't do it. "Is it time to get supper?"

His eyes moved from her to the bed. Desire flashed in them, but instead of acting on it, he asked, "Beth, could we go for a walk later? Just you and me? I'd like to talk to you about something. And if we don't plan it, Shannon and Wayne's munchkins will make sure we don't get two minutes alone."

He was going to tell her. On his own. Without her asking. "Sure. I promised Roger I'd play a game or two of beach tennis with him."

Nash crossed to her. "I promised Davie and Jason I'd help them fly a kite. They can't sit still for a minute."

His desire was alive and burning again. He played with her blouse collar. She felt she should back away until they talked, but when his hands roamed over her breasts, her reserve crumbled. As the cotton shaped to her, the heat from his touch was more scorching than an August sun. She steadied herself, trying to bury her suspicions that Nash was in her room for unethical reasons.

He brushed his lips across her forehead.

She murmured, "Nash, we shouldn't . . ."

"Dinner's ready!" Shannon called.

Beth sighed with relief.

Digging her toes in the sand, Beth watched Nash reel in Jason and Davie's kite while Wayne supervised Roger. Nash had so much patience with the boys. He treated them with respect, as if every moment he spent with them was special. Was that because of Christy?

Black night was overtaking gray dusk. When the kites were packed in their cases and the boys and Wayne headed toward the house, Nash ambled over to Beth. He held out his hand to her. "Ready for a moon-lit stroll on the beach?"

"You don't want to sit for a while first?"

He pulled her up. "No. I want to walk and talk with you. I've been thinking about it all day."

She flipped off her sandals and hooked her hand through his arm. "Let's go."

They walked in silence, close to the edge of the water, letting the foam spritz on their calves as they squished their toes in the spongy sand. The screech of a lone sea gull pierced the night as the beams from the crescent moon flirted with the waves. Hundreds of pinpoints of light pierced the dark sky.

The peace and tranquility encompassed Beth as the salty breeze tossed through her hair and fanned it out around her face. She swung Nash's hand. "Do you feel the power?"

He looked out at the expanse of ocean. "I feel it here, I feel it in the sunset, I feel it when I finish a garden then stand back and watch it bloom and grow."

Nash understood. He valued what was beautiful and important and dear to her. They might be different in the ways they worked, in the ways they organized, in the ways they lived, but there was a bond, a connection, in the way they thought . . . and felt.

The salty mist clung to her bangs as she tried to see into his soul, to learn about his past, to see his pain, to convince him he could trust her.

She must have conveyed the right message. He drew her away from the water, back to the gradually shelving beach, unbuttoned his shirt, and laid it on the sand. They sat together facing the black magnificence of ocean and let the low roar of the waves, the soft mellow oblong of moonlight, and the warm gentle breeze work their calming magic. There was no one in sight, no human sound for miles.

Nash curled his arm around Beth's waist and stared straight ahead. "This is difficult for me to talk about."

Beth slackened against his shoulder. "Shannon told me you had a daughter and she drowned. Don't be angry with her. I pried it out of her."

He shifted, his restlessness apparent. "Because of the way I acted?"

"Yes." Beth tried to keep her tone even, but didn't quite manage it.

"You were hurt I didn't tell you."

She concentrated on an oyster shell buried in the sand. "Disappointed."

His hold tightened slightly. "But you didn't push or ask this afternoon."

"I wanted you to feel free enough to tell me yourself."

"I haven't told you because I'm trying to work beyond it. It hurts too damn much to stir it up." His voice was distant, removed, as if he didn't want to think about it, let alone talk about it.

"But it was stirred up this afternoon."

He let out a burdened sigh. "In spades. I'm usually not overprotective with the boys, but put them near water . . ."

His words trailed off with a tightness that told her he was fighting his emotions. He began slowly. "Christy was everything to me. Everything good and sweet and perfect. She had beautiful silky brown hair and sparkling green eyes and cheeks that were always rosy. Even after Monica and I began having problems, we never disagreed about Christy. She was our glue. I suppose that wasn't good."

His wistfulness curled around Beth's heart and she had to swallow the lump that rose in her throat. She laid her hand on his thigh. "From what I hear, it's not unusual for a married couple to center their life around their children."

His hand came up and he waved away the excuse. "It's not unusual, but it doesn't make for a strong marriage. I guess that's why when Christy died, ours fell apart. One of the reasons, anyway."

The silence between them wasn't easy. Common sense told Beth that Nash needed to talk about what had happened. His feelings were still so raw because he'd never released them. "Can you tell me what happened?"

She felt him take a deep breath and thought he might move away, but he didn't. "I went out of town for a few days. Monica took Christy swimming in our pool. Christy loved the water. She didn't want to get out, but Monica insisted. They were watching a video together when Monica fell asleep. The family room had a door that opened onto the patio. From what we can piece together, Christy let herself out, managed to open the unlocked gate at the pool, and got in by herself."

Beth felt his shudder. "Monica found her in the deep water."

Nash's body was tense, stiff, as if he didn't control every muscle, he wouldn't control any. His sexy, strong, exciting exterior hid vulnerability. She could accept that. But could he accept her knowing it was there, or worse, seeing it?

She knew she was taking a risk but suspected Nash needed something no one had done for him. She turned, wrapped her arms around him, and held him tight. "You can let it go, Nash. Just let go."

When she stroked his back, he dropped his head on her shoulder.

"Being strong doesn't mean not feeling," she murmured. "It doesn't mean holding pain in."

He trembled and she held him tighter.

Waves pounded to the shore. A foghorn blew in the distance. Time sifted around and over them without touching them. Beth could feel Nash's anguish, the sadness and loneliness that reminded him his daughter was gone. Nothing she could say would take it away. Only time could do that. And maybe her love.

Eventually, he raised his head. She leaned back and ran her thumb over the tears on his cheek. He wouldn't look at her but merely stared over her shoulder. "I feel foolish."

"There's no reason to. Men need to be held as much as women."

He shook his head. "Society doesn't accept that."

"To hell with society."

He finally gazed into her eyes. "I didn't embarrass you?"

She held his face between her palms. "I respect a man who can let himself feel. I respect him even more if he can share what he's feeling."

He covered her hands with his, lifted one to his lips, and kissed her palm. Then he lowered them to his lap. "I'm not as strong as I like to believe," he confessed. "The end of my marriage made me feel less of a man, impotent in my ability to relate to a woman. I closed off a part of myself to protect it. But I hid it so far inside, I lost it. You've helped me find it again."

"I'm glad." She didn't say any more because she sensed he had something else to say.

"You know, I practiced being unflappable all my life. With my dad when he drank because someone had to be in charge, with my mother so she didn't know I was afraid I'd let her down. I got really good at it until it was part of me. Maybe if I'd been less unflappable, less strong, Monica would have seen I was as devastated as she was when Christy died."

"You didn't talk about it?" The silence answered her before he did.

He seemed to have to push out the explanation and the memories he wanted to forget. "No. We both blamed ourselves, we blamed each other. I thought it was my duty to be stolid, logical, reasonable. I set aside the possibility I could fall apart. I not only denied my feelings to her, I denied them to myself. Before we

split, she called me cold and unfeeling. I'd thought I
was being steady and dependable."

Beth was intensely aware of the hurt he'd experienced, the blow to his self-esteem. "I don't know what
to say."

He put his hand on her nape under the fall of her
hair. "You don't have to say anything. Your listening
is enough."

His touch sent tremors down her back. "Anytime,
Nash. Whenever you want to talk, I'm here."

"That's true for me, too."

Nash's sharing elevated their relationship to a new
plane. He trusted her. She wanted to trust him, too.
She'd tell him about John. But not now. She didn't
know how he'd take it. Besides, what was the loss of
her self-esteem compared to the loss of a child? Right
now she needed to be there for Nash. Her problems
could wait.

But how long? Sooner or later he'd find out about
her past. These things had a way of cropping up when
least expected. And then what?

Intuitively she knew neither of them could have a
shallow fling, not and face the mirror in the morning.
But serious could still mean temporary. Serious didn't
always lead to forever. And she suddenly realized that's
what she wanted with Nash. Forever.

That realization raised the stakes irrevocably and
made her even more protective of the love she was
feeling.

Nash encircled her with his strong arms. She lifted
her head and met his lips in a kiss that was ineffably
sweet, infinitely loving, temptingly giving. As the kiss
increased in fervor, Nash's hands slipped under Beth's
top and pulled it up.

She pulled away. "Nash, we can't."

"No one's around for miles." He unhooked her bra

and stroked her back. "It's just you and me, and I want to love you. I need you, Beth."

She couldn't deny him this. She couldn't deny herself. "I need you, too."

They undressed each other slowly, stretching out the pleasure, guided by each other's breathless murmurs. Nash became more earnest, his hands rougher, his kisses more demanding.

He laid her back on the sand and just stared. "I love looking at you."

Anticipation trembled in her voice. "I like you touching me even more."

He ran his finger around her nipple. "Like that?"

"Mmm. Yes."

He lowered his head and traced his tongue over the skin where his fingers had touched. "And that?"

His tongue was hot, wet, rough, erotic. A shower of fire pricked her breast and sped to her womb. "I love that."

He kissed around her navel and rubbed his chin in the downy hair below. His head dipped lower.

The firestorm tingled until her whole body quaked. "Nash."

"It's going to feel good, baby. So good. Trust me."

She did.

His tongue slipped into her folds, flicking, taunting, driving her crazy. The sand scraped her shoulders as she writhed and tried not to arch toward him wantonly. But the sensations were too overwhelming for her to stay still. Her hands went to his back and she clutched his shoulders, her nails digging into his skin. She felt the goose bumps break out on his arms right before his tongue sent her soaring and she climaxed.

Moments later, Nash stretched on top of her. The iron strength of his need probed her belly. He rubbed his body sensually against hers, their skin sticking, releasing, contacting, exciting.

Nash rose up. The moon illuminated his face. The angles and lines were taut with need, his eyes fierce with passion. With one smooth thrust he entered her. Seized by her desire, she tugged on him to drive deeper, but he pulled out.

"Stop teasing me. I want you."

He slid in and out again. "I'm not teasing. I'm prolonging."

When he drove in again, she caught him in her arms and nipped his shoulder. He chuckled and moved within her. She tightened, released, tightened, released until he sighed. "Each time I think it can't be any better. And it is."

He lay still, his breathing shallow as her hands massaged his head and she squeezed him tighter with her thighs. He kissed her arm, her shoulder, then homed in on her lips.

His mouth crushed hers and his tongue's hungry swirling had her clutching his lean flanks. She was drowning in an ocean of sensual delight. She broke away to kiss his face. His skin was hot under her lips and she could feel the tiny lines that gave it vitality and character. She moved beneath him in an age-old sorcery of motion that made him greedier to possess her. He thrust more vigorously, calling the rhythm, driving with the pounding of the surf, invading Beth's being until she accepted the volcanic eruption that wracked her body in tide after tide of rippling pleasure.

She wanted to shout, *I love you,* but held back. Soon she'd tell him that, too.

The night breeze cooled Nash's heated, damp skin as he recovered from their loving. Beth's vibrancy and beauty reminded him of a Tropicana rose. The florid orange-rose color that stood out anywhere, a floral scent that he could liken to an ancient Siren's song, softness so delicately feminine it almost hurt to touch it. Whenever he looked at her, the earth moved. It was damned unsettling. She drove him wild.

He was learning more about her. Her sighs, her shivers, her pleasures. A stroke along her neck and she quivered, a pass over her hip and she sighed, a gentle kneading of her breast and she softly moaned.

Pleasing her was always his initial aim. But he ended up losing control, getting greedy, being engulfed by a force more potent than he wanted to admit. He was frightened by the depth of his feeling. She was becoming his world.

She'd been so tender and compassionate about Christy. So accepting. He hadn't realized how much he needed that, how much he needed to talk about his daughter and let the emotions flow. Ingrained in him was an innate reluctance to discuss his feelings that had come from growing up too soon, too fast. He'd never let them loose with anyone.

He trusted Beth. But she still didn't trust him. He'd given her an opening and she hadn't taken it. He'd been so tempted to tell her he knew her past, yet he didn't want her to feel betrayed. He didn't want to spoil what they had. But could their relationship be based on anything but complete honesty?

TEN

Beth's car grunted, sighed, sputtered, and died. She banged her fist against the steering wheel, frustrated but not surprised. The engine had given her nothing but trouble for the last two months. Thank God, she was sitting at a stop sign rather than a stop light.

For the next few minutes as she turned the key in the ignition, she cooed, cajoled, and pleaded as if the vehicle was a recalcitrant pet. But it wouldn't respond. With a resigned sigh, she flicked on the flashers and jumped out. She'd just have to leave it while she called the auto club from the Handy Mart a half block away. She also called Nash.

He arrived a few minutes after the tow truck. By then, Beth was steaming. As Nash came up beside her, she said, "Would you believe drivers thought I was sitting there for my health? They honked, gestured, swore. What was I supposed to do? Get out and push it?"

The tow truck lifted the front end of the car.

Nash pushed his sunglasses on top of his head. "You could have stood next to the car and hiked up your skirt. You would've gotten plenty of help."

She glared at him. "How can you suggest such a chauvinistic—"

He knocked his shoulder against hers. "You've got legs to make a man drool. Never mind your eyes, your hair . . ."

She wasn't sure if she wanted to grin or keep on frowning. "Are you trying to make me angry enough to forget I have to pump more money into that heap and my mom and dad are probably sitting on my front step wondering where I am?"

"Nah. I'm trying to seduce you."

She burst into giggles. "You're good, Winchester. But not that good."

"Oh, yeah?" He caught her to him and kissed her until her hands twined around his neck and restless desire rose up to overtake her.

He lifted his head. "Am I good?"

Her words were a bit breathless. "You're awesome."

He kissed the tip of her nose and sighed deeply with the recognition that they couldn't go any further here. "Do you want to stop at the garage before I take you home?"

He could make her lose her head completely. Was it good to give a man that much power over her? She couldn't answer that question, but she could answer his. "No. I'll call them."

Nash checked his watch. "I have an appointment in an hour. I can probably wrap up business by five o'clock. Does that give you enough time with your parents?"

"That's plenty of time to catch up on news."

"I'm looking forward to meeting them. Are you sure you don't want to go to a nice restaurant instead of to a flea market?"

She saw the uncertainty in his eyes and realized the self-confident, strong Nash Winchester wanted to make a good impression. She had to make it clear her folks were ordinary people who would accept him because she did.

"Mom loved it the last time she was here. Flea markets are one of her hobbies. And Pops likes the selection of foods—especially the sausage sandwiches, the funnel cakes and the soft ice cream. They're bringing a cooler so they can take Lancaster-grown products back with them."

Nash's features relaxed; his lean cheeks losing their tautness. "It sounds like they know how to appreciate simple pleasures."

"They do."

He ran his thumb over her chinline. "So do you. Our picnic in bed last night was better than dinner in a four-star restaurant."

"Joe's deli makes great hamburger subs."

"I was more influenced by the company and the dessert." He wiggled his brows and his eyes twinkled with passionate mischief.

She felt herself blush. They'd fed each other, licked crumbs from bare skin, shared cheesecake kisses. She'd let a cherry drop provocatively on her breast then . . . When Nash touched her, caressed her, made love to her, she felt wild, abandoned, free. And he always encouraged her.

"You'll have to settle for doughnuts or apple dumplings tonight."

"Or wait until your parents go to their motel. Then we can see if there are any leftovers from last night."

She loved having Nash stay with her. She felt equally at home at his house. Actually, she felt good anywhere as long as she was with him. She couldn't imagine life without him.

As Nash drove to her apartment, he asked, "Have

you thought about buying a new car instead of getting yours fixed again?''

"Not seriously. I hate owing money. I just finished paying back—'' She stopped.

"A loan?''

Her stomach muscles clenched. "Yes.''

"On your car?''

"No. It had to do with the business.''

Nash gave her a scrutinizing look, but she didn't elaborate. She'd meant to tell him about John last night, but she'd felt so carefree, so happy. And she was afraid of the disbelief she might see in his eyes, or, worse yet, condemnation she didn't deserve. And if she saw that, she was terrified their relationship would never be the same.

"You wouldn't have to take out a loan. I could give you the money.''

Her brows furrowed and she wondered if he'd lost his mind. "For a car?''

"Sure.'' His leg moved from the accelerator to the brake and back. "You could get whatever you want—''

He was serious. "No. Absolutely not. That's worse than a loan. I'd feel beholden.''

He stopped for the car in front of him, waiting until the driver turned left. "That's an old-fashioned word.''

"Maybe I am old-fashioned in some ways.''

"You accepted the roses I brought you, and the chocolates.''

"Not cars. I don't want to feel . . . kept. And I won't put myself in a position to be ridiculed.''

He shifted his gaze from the road to her. "By whom?''

"By anybody who knows I can't afford to buy a new car!''

"No one *has* to know.''

That's what she'd once thought. She'd thought peo-

ple minded their own business because they were busy
with their own lives. But she'd found out differently.
"People talk, Nash. I'm not going to be food for that."
Not ever again.

"So you live your life according to what outsiders
think?" He sounded incredulous, as if he'd never expect that of her.

"Of course not."

"It sounds that way to me."

"You don't understand."

"Help me try."

She didn't know how to explain the turmoil, the
chaos that had been brought on by the scandal. "We
don't live in a vacuum. What we do affects others."

"I don't see how my giving you a car affects anyone
else."

"It affects the way I think about myself. I want to
make my own way." She could see Nash still didn't
understand. She touched his arm. "Thank you for your
offer. I appreciate it. But this is important to me. It has
to do with self-respect."

"I don't agree with your position. But I'll accept
it."

That's one of the qualities she loved about Nash.
Even if he didn't agree with her, he accepted her.

When Nash pulled up in front of her apartment, no
one was waiting. "I guess they're running late. Pops
probably saw something interesting and they stopped."

Nash unfastened his seat belt and shifted in his seat
to face her. "I'm glad you called me instead of a cab."

She laughed. "I knew you'd be more dependable."

He took her hand in his. "I mean it, Beth. It makes
me feel good that you depend on me."

"I haven't wanted to depend on anyone for a long
time." She squeezed his palm. "Relying on you feels

right. I don't lose who I am. You let me be my own person.''

Nash leaned across the gearshift to give her a lingering, sweet kiss. When he settled back, he ran his fingers over the knuckles of the hand he was still holding. ''You have lovely hands. Expressive hands. They can make me crazy with wanting you.''

His words could do the same thing as one of his kisses. Combine them, and her knees shook even though she was sitting. Attempting to defuse the steamy atmosphere, she stroked his forearm. ''And you have strong arms that make me feel safe . . . protected. It's a nice feeling.''

Realizing she was trying to put a lid on their passion, he chuckled. ''Tonight do we shoot for crazy or nice?''

''Tonight, we can shoot for both.''

Nash's lopsided smile said he approved. ''I'll be back as soon as I can. Enjoy your visit. Is there anything I should know before I see your parents?''

''Nervous?''

His shoulders rose and fell. ''Not exactly. But I don't want to make any gaffes.''

''Just be yourself. And don't take Pops too seriously. He likes to joke around.''

Beth remembered her comment to Nash as she brought her parents glasses of iced tea. Pops had been in her living room for almost an hour and had hardly teased her at all. That wasn't like him.

He ran a hand over his balding head and exchanged a look with his wife.

Beth set the tray of glasses on the coffee table. ''Okay, you two. What's going on?''

Marie nodded to her husband as if to say, ''Let's get this out of the way so we can enjoy our visit.''

In response, Cliff Terrell crossed his arms over his

potbelly and gave his daughter an apologetic smile. "Darlin', sit down. We have something to discuss with you."

"Why do I have the feeling I don't want to hear this?" Beth chose the swing chair so she didn't have to sit still.

Her father's eyes gentled, reminding her of the time she'd been cut from the basketball team and he found her crying on her bed. "Now, it's nothing bad. Just something you need to think about and maybe take care of."

"Don't talk the whole way around the country, Cliff. Get to the point," his wife scolded.

Beth's heart started beating faster despite her father's reassurance. "Somebody tell me!" She pushed against the floor with her toes.

Her father cleared his throat. "John called us."

Beth nearly jumped out of her chair. "John? Called you?"

"Yes, he wanted to—"

"How dare he—?"

"Now, let me finish. He wanted to talk to me."

Her voice was icy. "You didn't, of course. He did enough damage to all of us."

Cliff's apologetic expression deepened. "Once upon a time, Katie, I liked and respected John Winston. I never would have brought him home from the tavern and introduced him to you otherwise."

"I don't understand why—"

"I had to see if I'm as poor a judge of character as I was beginning to think I was."

Beth moved from the swing to sit on the arm of the sofa next to her dad, battling her anger to assuage her father's feelings of self-doubt. "Pops, you're a great judge of character. Neither of us realized how John was using us, that's all."

Her mother shook her head. "Honey, you can't get cynical because of this."

Beth studied her mother—her brown hair untouched by gray, her face only very lightly lined. Maybe it was her attitude that kept her young. She was always optimistic, determined to think the best of anyone. "I'm not cynical, just cautious these days."

Cliff patted Beth's arm. "John's not a bad man, darlin'. He was desperate. He wanted out of his marriage for years and he didn't have the guts to start a new life or rock the boat. We inadvertently handed him the opportunity by opening our home to him as a retreat from the pressures he felt coming from all sides. The more time he spent with us, the more his wife suspected he was having an affair. He didn't mean to drag you through the mud."

Not at first, maybe, but he'd done a hell of a good job of it. She thought back to the beginning in an attempt to understand her father's apparent about-face. When Beth had first met John, he'd been the perfect friend. He'd listened to her hopes and dreams about finding a man to love, her professional goals, her plans for her life. And she had listened to him.

"Then why did he let his wife think he was unfaithful with me to get out of the marriage? The whole idea was crazy."

"You could have made a public statement," Cliff stated for the umpteenth time since the story broke.

"Nobody would have believed me. Besides, I knew how unhappy John was." Her thoughts drifted again, this time to hours spent riding through the country with John, long walks in tall grass, evenings in Pop's tavern when she'd thought John was her friend.

Wistfully, she said, "You taught me loyalty, Pops. At the time, I thought keeping quiet was the best way to go."

Her mother said quietly, "And you were right. Because you did it for a friend."

She'd given John compassion, encouragement, loyalty, because that was the way she'd been raised. But now? What were her parents asking?

"You were John's best friend for over a year. He talked to your father because he's worried about you. He wants to see you." Her mother's voice was calm, soothing.

Beth stood and went to stare out the front window. The sun bounced off the maple leaves, turning the leaves to silver. "He sent me a letter asking me to meet him."

"It might be a good idea," her mother said tentatively, but Beth could tell she'd thought about the possibility long and hard.

"How can you say that? I don't want anything more to do with him. The loan's paid off. We're finished."

Cliff shook his head. "That's the point. We don't think you are. You haven't faced John since the day the paper came out with a picture of the two of you on the front page. It's not like you to avoid unfinished business."

Beth sighed. "What good would it do?"

Her mother's answer was quick. "You could go on with your life. Tell John how much he hurt you, how you felt. Yell, scream, do whatever you have to."

Beth plopped down on the floor, sitting Indian-fashion. "I *am* going on with my life. I have Nash—"

"Do you love him?" her mother asked, her head tilted inquisitively, inviting further confidences.

The answer when it came felt unshakably right. "Yes."

"Does he know about the scandal?" Marie asked.

Beth couldn't control the wave of fear that rolled over her. "No." She couldn't explain. She didn't know how to. Her feelings for Nash were tied to some elusive hope that her past didn't matter.

Cliff sat forward, his hands capping his knees. "You have nothing to be ashamed of, Katie darlin'. Why haven't you told him?"

"Because I'm afraid he won't understand," she blurted.

Cliff opened his mouth, but Marie put a calming hand on her husband's shoulder. "Does he love you?"

Beth played with the strings on her sneakers. She'd been afraid to ask herself that question. "I don't know. He hasn't said."

"If he loves you, honey, he'll understand that you and John were friends."

Beth straightened her legs in front of her and stared at her mother meaningfully. "Will he? Look how many of my 'friends' didn't."

"Keeping it from him will only make it that much harder to tell him," Cliff offered.

"He'll wonder why," Marie added.

The silence was louder than anything else her parents could have said. Her mother finally spoke. "If you confront John, maybe you can really get on with your life."

"And start by telling Nash." Beth smiled as hope took root. She could already feel the burden beginning to lift.

Her father relaxed, leaning against the cushion. "You could come down next weekend."

"Let me think about it."

The open air flea market bustled with activity. Proprietors sold everything from lemonade to sweatshirts. But all the activity didn't mask the fact that Cliff Terrell's eyes were on Nash as he fed Beth a French fry and tenderly wiped the salt from her lips.

Nash understood. The man was protective of his daughter. Clifford Terrell wore a jovial face and joked like a pro, but he was watchful and nothing slipped his notice. He'd listened to Nash's every word and watched his daughter's reactions. Nash knew he'd be the same way if Christy had lived to— No, now wasn't the time to think about Christy, Nash thought as he watched Beth move beside her mother to search through a table of genuine leather pocketbooks. Now was the time to think about the future . . .

The future that was approaching fast as Cliff Terrell stuffed his hands into the pockets of his plaid shorts and stopped next to Nash. "Beth tells us you do the same kind of work she does."

Was this where he was supposed to declare his intentions? He hoped not. He wasn't sure exactly what his intentions were just yet. There was still the matter of John Winston to discuss with Beth. "That's right."

"She also says your work is known all over the country and you're very successful."

"That's true."

Cliff's brows lifted owlishly. "I admire a man who can admit his worth." He took a pack of gum from his pocket and flicked a piece into his palm. He offered one to Nash, and at his refusal pocketed it again. "Marie made me give up cigars for this. She said she wants to make sure I'm around as long as she is."

"Women catch on faster than men."

Cliff eyed him thoughtfully. "Beth would have my head for this, but I want to know how you feel about her." He popped the stick of gum into his mouth, his gaze narrowing.

Nash met his eyes steadily. "I care about her a great deal."

"She's not just one in a string, someone to keep you from being bored?"

"No, she's not." Nash heard the defensive note in his voice and banished it. He continued evenly. "I respect her and would never do anything to hurt her."

It was true. More and more Nash was coming to face his feelings for Beth. He was realizing he wanted a second chance at a wife and a family. This time he'd do it right. The woman made the difference. The way he felt about Beth made the difference. He was a different person when he was with her. A better person. A complete person.

Beth's father gave him a probing stare, then nodded as if satisfied with what he found.

The four of them wove in and out of the market maze, dodging kids and adults, stopping to buy produce from a Mennonite woman, a round of cheddar cheese from an Amish dealer dressed in black, his wide-brimmed hat pulled low over his brow.

Beth took the cheese from her mother and inserted it in one of the shopping bags Nash was carrying. "If we want to go to the dry-goods auction, we'd better take this stuff to the car. Some of it needs to go in the cooler."

Cliff said, "No use for all of us to go. Katie, you can help me. Your mom and Nash can get us seats."

Beth's head jerked up at her father's use of her pet name, and she snatched a look at Nash. "Pops used to call me Katie when I was little. Katherine's my first name."

Nash kept his expression bland. "It's a pretty name."

Before he could say anything else, Beth took the bags from him and handed them to her father. "Let's get these to the car. We don't want to miss any bargains."

As Beth and Cliff started off toward the parking lot, Nash and Marie headed for a large cement-block building. Nash let Marie pass in front of him. "Beth said you've been here before."

Marie stepped over the threshold and looked over the rows and rows of chairs, merchandise stacked against the side walls, and the platform up front where the auctioneer stood at a microphone. "Several times. This place amazes me. I love the bustle and activity. And I've never seen anything like this auction. You never know what he's going to sell."

Nash moved as a couple brushed past him to look for seats up front. "I heard the auctioneer gets his bulk quantities from companies that go out of business or trucks that are in accidents."

"That's right. I bought casserole dishes and generic shampoo last time. I can't wait to see what he puts up tonight."

Marie had Beth's enthusiasm for life. It manifested itself in her walk; it glowed in her eyes. Nash guided her to four seats in the back of the auction house. He sat down next to her and listened to the hawker describe the merits of a hair dryer.

Marie's arm brushed his. "You know, don't you?"

Nash hid his surprise. "Know?"

Marie's eyes, the same deep brown as Beth's, passed over his face relentlessly. "You didn't even blink when Cliff called Beth Katie."

Nash didn't know what to do. If she was guessing, if she told Beth before he could that he knew . . . He didn't want to lie. "I'm not sure I know what you're referring to."

"Beth's been through a lot. It's hard for her to open up these days." Marie swerved her gaze to the front as if to give him time to think about her words.

He sighed. Marie's invitation was subtle but unmistakable. If he wanted to know the truth, he could get it from her. But did he want to learn it that way? "Beth hasn't told me much about her past. I want her to trust me enough to tell me herself but . . ." Nash raked his long fingers through his hair. "I have a lot of questions."

Marie cocked her head and said gently, "I imagine you do."

Nash moved in his chair and rubbed the back of his neck. "I don't understand why she became involved."

The last rays of sun shining through a high, elongated window revealed the same red highlights in Marie's short cut as in Beth's curls. "It's complicated. But since you want to hear the story from her, why don't you simply ask her about it instead of wondering and guessing?"

He gave an exasperated shrug. "I want her to trust me enough to confide in me."

Marie shook her head wisely. "You're playing a dangerous game, Nash. You could lose her."

He nodded solemnly. "You could be right. I've been thinking about that a lot lately."

Marie's knowing look said he better think about it more.

Beth waved to her parents as their car pulled away from the curb. She went inside and found Nash waiting for her on the sofa with a bag on his lap.

He ignored her puzzled look. "It's a shame your parents couldn't stay longer."

"Pops doesn't like to be away from the tavern too long. He thinks they'll lose business if he's not there. Actually, I think he misses talking to all the people who come in." She pointed to the bag on his lap. "What's that?"

He grinned. "Come look."

Crossing to him, she took the bag from his lap and peeked inside. She pulled out a silky, deep-purple teddy. "Nash, it's lovely. But why . . . ?"

He stood. "I noticed you like to wear those to bed. And since you won't accept a car, I bought the next best thing."

She held it up to her shoulders. "Want me to put it on?"

"We could go to the bedroom and discuss it." He traced his fingers over her lips.

She parted them and tasted his finger with her tongue. Erotic energy rebounded between them. The passion flashing in his eyes took her breath away. He put his arm around her and led her to the bedroom.

Nash stepped out of his Docksiders and unzipped his shorts. "I like your parents."

Beth laid the teddy on the chair, tugged off her socks and sneakers, and pulled her knit top over her head. "They liked you. I could tell." The evening had gone well. But she had to tell Nash about next weekend. During the course of the evening, she'd made up her mind. Her parents gave good advice. "Uh, I have some business to take care of in Leesburg. So, I'm going down Saturday. I'll be back Sunday afternoon."

Nash went still. "Do you want me to come along?"

"No! I mean, we wouldn't have time together. I'm not going down until Saturday afternoon. It's only one night." Lord, she was rambling. He was going to get suspicious.

"I'll miss you," he said simply.

She stripped off the rest of her clothes quickly. "I'll miss you, too. Nash, it's not that I don't want you along. Some weekend soon we'll go down and spend it with my parents."

His eyes narrowed pensively. "But this is something you have to do alone."

"Yes."

He removed his shorts, then his shirt. "Does it affect us?"

Even if she'd still been dressed, she'd feel naked. "It might. Don't ask me questions, okay?"

"Beth." Her name was soft, hardly a whisper. He looked troubled.

"Nash . . ." Her eyes pleaded with him.

"All right. No questions. Not tonight." His eyes embraced hers until she trembled and stepped close to him. He took her in his arms for a tense moment. Their world was gray, hushed, murky because of words unsaid.

Nash's hands played up and down her back, sending rippling sensations coursing through her body. She found herself matching his motion by stroking his neck and shoulders. She leaned into his arms, needing to forget about the upcoming meeting, needing to chase away all the things she had to tell him. Luxuriating in the pressure of his thighs against hers, she turned toward the warmth of his breath on her neck. The longer he held her, the more she became aware of the changes occurring in their bodies—their accelerated heartbeats, their shorter breaths, their heat coalescing in a cloud around them.

Nash reached around her and clasped his hands. "Tonight the outside world doesn't exist. It's just you and me."

Relieved by the reprieve, she reached up around his neck, staring into his eyes. The heady smell of him disoriented her thoughts until she swayed into him, losing all sense of time and place.

Nash lowered his head and his parted lips blazed a path along her throat. "Do you know how exciting you are? How much I want to make love with you?"

His murmur echoed with the gravelly sensuality of

desire unfulfilled. He nipped at her lower lip and the persuasive insistence of his tongue caused a fluttering sensation in her stomach. He managed to convey such gentleness, tenderness, and passion in a single kiss. His hands pressed her tighter . . . tighter against him until she could feel the heated tumescence under the softness of his briefs. A moan lodged in her throat.

His hands left her back and wandered to the sensitive area of her stomach. She reciprocated by tangling her fingers in the soft swirls of his chest hair. He could activate such impatience in her, such a need to be fulfilled.

He must have felt it because he mumbled into her ear. "Let's move to the bed."

Nash stripped. They lay on their sides, facing each other. He stroked her face, lingering over each feature. When he placed gossamer-light kisses where his fingers had touched, she trembled. Brushing his fingertips over her mouth, he followed them with a taunting kiss that imitated and foretold of the pleasure to come. After a detour to her shoulder, he found her mouth again and danced his fingers over her rib cage.

Beth's hands moved restively from Nash's corded shoulder muscles to the exploration of the breadth of his back and the nubs of his spine. She wanted to tell him how much she loved him. But not yet. Soon. Sunday night. She wanted the past settled. She wanted to be free of it. Instead of telling Nash she loved him, she satisfied herself by provocatively touching his lips with her tongue and rubbing her breasts against his chest. His deep indrawn breath excited her with the knowledge that she could arouse him to the same tingling pitch she was experiencing.

Nash kneaded her buttocks, pressing her against his arousal. When her passion flared in her eyes, he pulled her leg over his hip and took a deep, long kiss that led to another . . . and another. Their touching, reaching, yearning, became urgent and desperate. Fusion was hot and explosive. Nash pulled back, then drove in deeper.

Beth abandoned herself to the tide of love that washed over her. Undulation after undulation of escalating pleasure had her clasping Nash tighter, begging him to knife deeper, arching into each of his thrusts until she climbed to the tip of the highest wave. She emitted a cry as old as womanhood. It was the catalyst that brought Nash to a trembling release.

ELEVEN

Nash stood in Shannon's kitchen Saturday evening, grinning like a besotted adolescent, "What do you think?"

Shannon's "ooh" of approval when she took the small velvet box from his hand reassured him his choice had been a good one. "I don't know about Beth, but I wouldn't mind having one of these. A heart-shaped diamond ring. Am I crazy or does it have a blue tint?" She turned the box so the light hit the ring at various points.

"It's a blue diamond. Different, like she is. Do you think she'll like it?"

Shannon closed the box and handed it back to him. "I don't think the ring's the issue. If you're going to propose, do you think she'll accept?"

He'd wanted to chase after Beth this weekend, follow her, and find out if the trip had anything to do with John Winston. Intuition told him it did. His stomach turned over. Was she going to return home and tell him they were finished? He couldn't believe that. He couldn't believe Beth would have taken their relationship this far if she didn't love him. But why hadn't she said it?

He hadn't told her he loved her, either. After she'd left today, he'd realized that was a mistake. Maybe if she knew how he felt, she would have changed her plans this weekend. Instead of kicking himself over and over, impulsively he'd gone out and bought the ring. Tomorrow night she'd know exactly how he felt. He loved her. He wanted to marry her. He wanted to have children with her. He wanted to grow old with her.

But what did she want?

"Nash?" Shannon brought him back to the present.

He pocketed the ring and stifled the edginess caused by waiting. "Before I ask her, we're going to get everything out in the open."

"You're going to tell her you know about her past?"

"Yes."

"You look worried."

"I don't know how she's going to feel that I knew and didn't tell her."

"Can't you just not say anything?"

He gave her a measuring glance. "No. We can't begin a marriage based on deception. I hate secrets and this one's killing me. I never should have tried to elicit her trust by keeping quiet."

Shannon stretched on her tiptoes and lifted the cake holder down from the top of the refrigerator. "I don't know what you think Beth's done, but if what you know is true, can you handle that?"

"I can handle anything if it means we have a future together."

Her smile curved in a soft arc as she set the holder on the table and lifted the lid. "You really love her."

"I love her. And I need her. As much as I need air to breathe. She's sunshine and flowers and hope."

Shannon contemplated him for a few moments. "You haven't known her long—a month, six weeks."

Her comment surprised him. "I don't need six months or a year to know her, or to know how I feel about her."

"Isn't she the first since Monica?"

"Yes."

"Are you sure you don't have feelings piled up that need to come out and she's available?"

He leaned against the counter. "Shan, aren't you happy for me? What are you trying to do?"

"I like Beth." Opening a drawer, she removed a knife to cut the chocolate cake. "I'm simply playing devil's advocate. This is a big step."

Trust had always been a problem for Shannon, too. Because of their father's irresponsible behavior, it had been difficult for her to trust men. She'd dated Wayne for a year and had been engaged for another year before she finally agreed to set the date.

Nash tried to keep the impatience from his voice. "I don't need more time or to date a dozen more women to know Beth and I are right together."

She sighed and removed a pack of paper plates from the cupboard. "I'm not trying to project my fears onto you. I just don't want you to get hurt."

"It wouldn't be the first time. If I do get hurt, it's my own fault. Beth and I should have had a discussion weeks ago. I should have gotten everything out in the open. Now, I will."

She looked over her shoulder. "It's not your responsibility alone."

He pushed away from the counter, skimmed his finger along the bottom edge of the cake to gather icing. "I know. But sometimes one person has to take the lead. If I'd opened up with Monica, suggested we get counseling, maybe the marriage wouldn't have fallen apart. Somebody has to take the risk first. If it has to be me, so be it.''

Shannon slapped his hand. "You've changed. From the first day you met Beth, I could see it happening.''

He licked his finger and grinned. "For better or worse?''

"Better. You laugh more, you're relaxed even when you're not with the kids. And you're not working so much or keeping such a slavish schedule.'' She grinned back. "One could say you've become more flexible.''

"One could stop looking so smug.''

Shannon's impudent smirk reminded him of when they were kids and she'd stick out her tongue at him. Before he could counterattack, Wayne came into the kitchen carrying Davie.

Wayne nodded to Nash in greeting, then turned to address his wife. "Hon, his nose is still running and he has a low-grade fever. Where did you put the liquid Tylenol?''

Shannon immediately went to feel the back of Davie's neck and kiss his forehead. "It's on the top shelf of the medicine cabinet.''

Wayne left with Davie, Shannon's eyes following their every step. Nash knew she worried incessantly where the kids were concerned. "It'll pass, Shan. It's just a cold,'' he offered gently.

She turned to him as if surprised she was so transparent. "He caught it because he's with fifteen other kids in day-care.'' Shannon gnawed on her bottom lip. "Maybe I should check around for someone who keeps two or three kids in her house. I didn't have much time and this day-care center had such a good reputation . . .''

Wayne and Davie returned in time to hear her last comment. Davie rubbed his nose with his wrist. "Uncle Nash, I made friends. Lots of them.''

Nash held out his hands and lifted Davie from Wayne's arms. "I bet you did. Do they know how to play marbles?"

"I'm teachin' Jenny, but she's not as good as Beth."

Nash rumpled Davie's hair and gave the boy a hug.

Wayne took Shannon by the shoulders. "He loves it at day-care. It's good for him to socialize with somebody other than his brothers. So stop worrying." He gave her a quick squeeze, then turned to Nash. "Will you look in on them next weekend? I have to go to an exhibit in Minneapolis. I hope to make contacts for when I start the business."

"Sure. No problem. Shannon knows she can count on me."

Shannon poked her husband's chest with her index finger. "You call *me* a worrier. The kids and I can take care of ourselves."

He caressed her chin. "I know. But I hate leaving. I hope this is the last time."

Nash understood. His profession would never come before his marriage or family again.

Beth stood at her parents' white picket fence and watched John's BMW zoom down the road away from their house. Conflicting emotions taunted her. She'd probably never see him again. That was her purpose in coming and she'd thought that was what she wanted.

But when she saw him and remembered the closeness and warmth they'd shared . . .

A hand on her shoulder startled her. "How did it go?" her mother asked with concern.

Beth looked over the acreage surrounding the house. "Let's walk."

The sun was making a slow descent as they rambled through the grass. "He's aged, Mom. So much. He looks sixty instead of fifty. Somehow, since I thought everything that happened was what he wanted, I assumed he'd had an easy time of it. But I was wrong. He was uprooted, too. Even though he was tired of politics and marriage, both were familiar."

Her mother's stride matched hers. "There's comfort in familiarity. That's one reason why unhappily married couples stay married."

"That's basically what he said. Adjusting to not being married was as difficult as being unhappily married. But he's thankful he's out."

Marie stopped. "Was he trying to win your sympathy?"

Beth kicked a loose stone with the toe of her sneaker. "No. He was being factual. Most of our conversation was factual. Until I told him how much his betrayal hurt. I couldn't hold it in, Mom. I was going to be cold, objective. But I ended up crying."

"There's nothing wrong with that, honey. It's about time he knew what you went through."

Beth started walking again. "He knows. And he realizes we can't be friends again. But I told him we're not enemies, either. I understand how trapped he felt. He knows he was a coward and he got his divorce at my expense. He offered me money—'for damages,' as he puts it. I told him to forget it. The other money was a loan; I paid it back. I don't want anything from him. I want to get on with my life."

She paused, then added, "I told him I forgive him."

Her mother regarded her reflectively. "Do you? Or did you say it to make him feel less guilty?"

Beth had asked herself the same question and come up with the right answer. "Yes, I do forgive him. And because I do, I feel at peace, and free. The past can't touch me now. When I get home tomorrow, I'm going to tell Nash. If he loves me, he'll believe me and none of it will matter."

"Nash is a reasonable man. It's long past time you and he had this talk."

Her mother sounded as if she knew something Beth didn't.

Sunday afternoon, the clock on Nash's desk was moving minute by slow minute and he was getting nothing productive done. He switched off the computer, closed the folder with projection estimates, and filed it in the cabinet. Opening the second drawer, he pulled out Osgood's file. Beth's was behind it.

With a sigh, he laid them down on his desk. The Osgood presentation was only a week away. He had to make sure his speech was in order. He glanced at the boards on the long table. They needed a few finishing touches but he couldn't concentrate.

Beth's file drew his eyes. There was no point opening it. He'd memorized its contents. Besides, what he'd told Shannon was the truth. None of it mattered. As soon as Beth returned, he'd tell her he knew, and they'd move on. Hopefully to a life together. He didn't want to consider the alternative.

He checked the clock again. Three P.M. He needed to do something physical to work off the tension. No jogging so . . . He crossed to the sliding-glass doors that led out back. The grass was lush and long. Yard work was just what he needed. Then a cold shower. Then a long talk and a romantic dinner with the woman he was going to marry.

Beth parked in Nash's driveway, wired and tense. She hadn't even stopped at her apartment. Jumping out of the car, thankful the new carburetor was working like a charm, she ran up to Nash's front door. He had given her a key, but she'd forgotten it. She rang the doorbell.

After a few minutes, she opened the door. "Nash? Nash? Are you home?" She hadn't taken the time to look in the garage to see if his car was there.

Recognizing the buzzing sound, she went to the dining room and stepped outside onto the redwood deck. The light wind carried the scent of freshly cut grass and baked earth. Nash was astride a riding mower. His T-shirt was plastered to his upper torso, marked by dark rows and circles of sweat. Sunlight bounced off his hair and glistening thighs.

She loved this man so. Did he want a commitment as much as she did? Were his feelings deeper than passion? If he didn't love her yet, would he in time?

When he rounded a corner to begin another row, he spotted her. Without hesitation, he drove straight toward the deck, cutting a diagonal path across the unmowed half of the yard.

Beth pushed away from the railing and walked down the steps. She waited on the flagstone patio as he motored to the edge, switched off the mower, and hopped off.

Beth's palms became sticky as he flipped off his sunglasses, laying them on the mower's seat, and stood in front of her. He looked so serious that she lost her voice and her heart beat triple time.

"Good trip?"

The sun was hot on her head as the breeze tossed a few curls across her cheek. "Yes."

Nash brushed the hair aside as his hypnotic green eyes combed her face. "The car work okay?"

She wanted to lean into his hand but didn't. Could he read the love in her heart? She wanted to give it to him, to hear him say he returned it. "Fine." The small talk was grating, but she didn't know how to switch gears.

His hand dropped and he looked down at his clothes.
"I have to get a shower, then we can talk."

She thought of the first shower they took together
and felt her skin begin to tingle. "Don't you want to
finish the yard?"

He watched her speculatively. "It can wait."

She attempted to pull off a casual shrug. "If you
want to finish, I don't mind."

"Beth . . ."

"Really, it's fine."

His demanding gaze wouldn't let her go. "We have
to have a *long* talk. I have a question to ask you."

Her stomach muscles clenched. Something was wrong.
"Ask."

"No. Not yet. I'll be in in about fifteen minutes."

Surprising her, he pulled her into his arms. His kiss
was hot, fast, probing . . . desperate. When he released
her, she stood stunned for a moment, the impression of
his body still burning her. He jumped astride the mower
and took off across the yard as if the devil was after
him.

Bemused, she opened the lower level doors and went
into Nash's office. She'd only been here a few times.
It was masculine and reflected his penchant for organization. The navy leather couch and chairs, the black
slate-topped tables, the icy-blue carpeting—all gave
a no-nonsense but comfortable ambience. She didn't
know how he kept his desk and drafting area so neat.
She knew the smaller adjoining room toward the front
of the house was his secretary's office and just as
orderly.

To pass the time, she drifted over to a table and
smiled. A set of boards was laid out side by side. Green
tape coded the corner of each board. Nash had shown
her his system. He labeled all material from each of
his clients with a different color of tape.

It wasn't until she had looked over the first board and glanced at the bottom that she realized this was Osgood's resort. Her boards were finished and she was satisfied she'd win the contract if her oral presentation went well. So she studied Nash's finished concept.

As she looked at the first one and then the second, her heart beat faster. Nash's concept was very much like hers. It also targeted age groups, but with a historical flavor—a section for couples taken from the Middle Ages with castle sculptures and a knight on a charger, a dinosaur land for children, an Olympic-theme circuit training path. The only specific difference was a miniature golf course with an Old West theme.

A suspicion formed in her mind before she could stop it as she remembered catching Nash looking at her boards that day at the shore. No. Nash wouldn't have copied her idea. They thought alike in many ways. That was all. She dismissed the similarity. Nash had never been anything but sincere and honest. Right?

Her eyes shifted to the desk and the folders there. Nash's printing was legible, neat, bold. The top folder bore her name.

She moved closer. Why would Nash have a folder concerning her? Unless . . . Could Rosenthal's suspicions have been right? Did Nash hire private investigators and do background checks? Had he done one on her?

Don't jump to conclusions, Beth. He's so organized, anything's possible.

She wiped one clammy hand on her shorts before she reached for the folder. Fear stabbed her chest as she picked it up. She opened it slowly. There were photographs of a few of the bigger projects she'd completed, and a computer printout listing landscapes, types of flowers, and plants, any unusual features. This information was public knowledge. Anyone could get it. Why had Nash wanted it? To decide if she was a serious threat? And if so, then what?

She flipped over the computer sheet and saw the clippings. Tears came to her eyes. Betrayal, intense and suffocating, overwhelmed her. Why? Why had he done this? The date on the printout showed he'd known for weeks. Why hadn't he told her?

Because he had a motive. Damn! She'd thought the serious discussion they were about to have had to do with their future. Hah! It probably had more to do with blackmail.

Her hopes died, and one tear after another ran down her cheeks. He was *using* her—stealing her ideas, pretending he cared about her, keeping her close to keep an eye on her. Sure, he didn't want her to get to know Osgood. She'd have an ''in'' and he wouldn't. The jealousy had been an act. And she'd fallen for it!

She'd also fallen prey to his lovemaking skills, his false honesty, his pretended sincerity. She looked down at the photograph of her and John. Was she so susceptible? Was she so naive that men saw her as an easy target? What was wrong with her? Giving compassion and friendship and accepting it in return, giving love and wanting to believe it was reciprocated—was that such an untenable goal?

The sliding-glass doors opened and closed. Beth raised her head, anger as tempestuous as a hurricane keeping her silent.

Nash approached, seeing the folder in her hand. ''I can explain that.''

The weight of what she'd found pushed her down. She fought her way back up. ''Sure you can. You can explain everything. You should have been an actor instead of an architect because you've given an Academy Award-winning performance!''

Her attack seemed to astound him. "Now, wait a minute."

She squared her shoulders. "No. *You* wait a minute." She threw the folder on the desk and waved to the table with his boards. "I suppose it's a coincidence that after you looked at my ideas, yours came out similar?"

He grimaced and stuffed his hands in his pockets. "You're jumping to conclusions, Beth."

"Am I? Tom Rosenthal warned me about you."

"Warned you?" Nash's eyes narrowed.

The accusations surfaced as if Rosenthal was whispering in her ear. "He told me you do whatever you can to discredit your competitors. He said you get friendly to learn whatever you can. And if that doesn't work, you hire an investigator to do a background check."

Nash swore under his breath. "That man has *some* imagination. I'd have to be as rich as Osgood to afford that."

Her fury erupted when she glared at her folder on his desk. "Then what in God's name is that? It proves what he said is true."

"It proves nothing of the sort. I don't know what Rosenthal's problem is, but he has a lousy attitude. It's no wonder he loses more projects than he wins."

"His attitude has nothing to do with his work."

"Sure it does. It colors it."

"Then why did Osgood ask him to bid?"

"Because his work is technically perfect even though it's uninspired." Nash scowled. "I don't know how you could believe a stranger—"

She impatiently cut him off, her hurt thrust aside so she could strengthen her defenses. "You were a stranger, too. And if he was so wrong, where did *that* come from?"

Nash's line of vision switched from her to the desk. "I have a friend."

"Who's a private investigator and you get a discount?"

He weighed her words. "Why do you want to think the worst?" His jaw clamped in a set position, his mouth compacted into a taut line.

She resented his seeming calmness when her world was falling apart. "Because I've been used before and I recognize the signs. I thought you were attracted to me, I thought we had some kind of . . . connection, I thought you respected me. But the whole time you were planning to blackmail me!"

"Blackmail? Have you gone off the deep end?" Nash took a step closer and planted his feet firmly apart.

"No. I'm waking up. I should have known better than to believe in fairy tales and whirlwind romances." Beth couldn't keep the bitterness out of her answer. "You moved too fast, buster. That should have warned me. You set out to make a good impression. When the powerful, well-known architect's polish didn't work, you convinced me you were a family man. And all the time you were setting me up! I was so stupid. I thought tonight was going to be . . . special. I never imagined blackmail."

Nash's anger seemed to coalesce in a cloud around him. He didn't attempt to hide the hard edge to his voice or the fire in his eyes. "You mentioned that word more than once. Since you've worked everything out, tell me what I was going to do."

"Use that information. Threaten me. If I don't give up the Osgood project, you'll go public with my past, bring it all up again. Well, it won't work. I won't drop the project. If Osgood finds out and I lose it, so be it. I'll go after something else. And if the information goes public again, I don't give a damn. This time I won't run. Gossip is gossip. And just like three years ago, it'll eventually lose steam. Now there's nothing to feed it and it'll come and go overnight. You underestimated me, Nash. I don't scare that easily."

He pushed his hand through his hair with agitation. "I underestimated you, all right. After what we've shared, how can you possibly believe I'd want to hurt you?"

To protect herself, she summoned her courage and began building walls by wrapping her response in sarcasm. "What did we share? Sex? Passion?"

His words flew out of his mouth like three separate cannon balls. "There was more."

Beth wanted to duck, turn away, evade his gaze so he couldn't see the truth. Calling on every ounce of self-respect, she blanked her expression and lied. "No. I got carried away by chemistry. That's all it was." It was difficult to draw a breath. Speaking so lightly of something she felt so deeply twisted her heart.

Nash took a few strides toward her. "Don't do this, Beth. Give me a chance—"

"To lie to me more?" She steeled herself against all the tender feelings, against the inclination to listen to his excuses. "You knew my background. You never gave a hint that you did."

"I was wrong," he said dully. "I should have told you I knew. But I wanted you to trust me—"

"So you could deceive me."

"Deceive? You want to talk about deceive?" he roared, his hand cutting through the air. "You're not even using your first name anymore!"

She wouldn't let him turn this around on her. She lifted her chin stubbornly.

He clenched his fists at his sides, and with a visible effort softened his voice. "Why didn't you tell me?

Were you so ashamed of what you did, you thought I couldn't forgive you?''

A chill tripped down her spine. "Forgive me? I don't need anyone's forgiveness. I didn't do anything wrong!" she exploded.

"Those articles are pretty complete and convincing. Places you were seen, how often Winston 'visited' you. Not to mention the photograph. How are you going to explain that away?''

"I don't have to explain anything."

"If it's not true, why didn't you defend yourself? You didn't make one public statement."

"Because I couldn't have changed anything. And by keeping quiet, I helped John free himself from an unhappy marriage and a career that was causing him enough stress for a heart attack at an early age."

Nash slanted her a glance, his eyes unreadable. "Are you saying you didn't have an affair with the man?"

How often had friends asked her that question with the same inflection of doubt? A poignant ache squeezed her heart. "It doesn't matter if I did or not. Not anymore. I was going to tell you about it tonight—all of it—and hope you would believe the truth. It was so important you believe me."

She shook her head. "I've been such a fool. You've been playing with me. You said it didn't matter if I won the contract. You were *so* blasé. And I lapped it up because I wanted to believe it."

"I have *not* played with you. I have *not* lied to you."

She glared at him.

He rubbed his hand across his temple. "All right. Maybe not telling you I knew was lying. But you sure as hell lied by omission, too. Where did you really go this weekend?''

"It doesn't matter. I thought I was putting the past behind me. Again, I was naive. I didn't think that someone unscrupulous like you would continue to use it against me.''

Nash's face flushed. ''You truly believe that I set up our relationship and had sex with you to gain your confidence, that I stole your ideas, and intended to blackmail you?''

''Yes.''

''And nothing I can say will change your mind.''

''No.''

He closed the distance between them. His nose was only inches from hers. She could feel his heat and suppressed anger, smell his maleness, taste his last kiss. His arm muscles tensed and she knew he was restraining himself from touching her.

For the first time since she met him, she felt intimidated as he said, ''You'll take the word of someone like Rosenthal instead of someone you've spent time with, talked to, and almost lived with for the past two weeks? I don't know what else you've done in your life, but *that's* gullible.''

Emotion surged through her so strong she could hardly stand to look at him. It hurt too much to remember kissing his lips, touching his body, lying in his arms. She moved away from him toward the steps.

''Beth.'' When she turned, he said, ''I was going to tell you I knew tonight. That's what I wanted to talk to you about. And I was going to ask you—''

''You expect me to believe you?''

''Yes, I do. I expect you to be reasonable and see how silly your accusations are.''

''Silly? I've told you before, don't patronize me. My accusations are about as silly as John using our friendship to get out of his marriage without regard for my reputation. As silly as me losing my job or not being able to walk down the street without people pointing, making snide comments, and judging when they have no idea what the facts are.'' Tears crowded her throat, then escaped and skittered down her cheeks in uneven tracks. "They're as silly as seeing my designs reflected in yours.''

Nash's eyes looked pained. His expression was grim. His voice was deceptively low with an undertone of frustration. "Think about something, Beth. Think about the night on the beach in Stone Harbor. Then you tell me what's between us isn't real.''

She took three heaving breaths to snuff a sob and regain control. "The night before the story broke, I had dinner with John. He knew that picture was coming out in the morning edition because a reporter had called him for an interview. John didn't tell me he confirmed the story, he didn't prepare me, he acted like a friend.'' She clasped her hands together tightly before continuing. "So . . . I believe you had a daughter. I believe she died and maybe you're still hurting. But I also believe if you wanted Osgood's contract badly enough, you could pretend what you didn't necessarily feel. It was a tactic to get me to trust you.''

Nash pulled back and became remote. "You have it all figured out. But you've missed one important fact. I am *not* John Winston and whatever he did to you has nothing to do with me except in your mind.''

The silence between them thundered as their eyes locked. Beth felt herself shaking and she knew she couldn't stay in the same room with him for another minute. She looked away and grabbed the banister.

"You're making a mistake, Beth.''

"My mistake was getting involved with you.'' She didn't look back as she climbed the steps, picked up her purse in the living room, and walked out of Nash's life.

TWELVE

When Beth shoved the bulky box to the high shelf in the closet of her spare room, it almost tumbled back down. The exertion of hoisting it into place again made her groan. Nobody in their right mind housecleaned in this heat. But then, who said she was in her right mind?

She'd worked like a dervish all week, spending long hours at the office, then cleaning windows, swiping at cobwebs, and polishing cabinets when she came home. Most of the week she'd achieved her goal—not thinking about Nash. The trouble was, her unconscious mind wasn't cooperating. Her dreams, stray thoughts, the resort designs, all effectively reminded her she was only fooling herself and she'd have to come to terms with her feelings eventually . . .

Probably tomorrow at one in Osgood's office when she had to face Nash. At least other people would be there and she could give him the cold shoulder without a confrontation. Her stomach knotted. Nerves. Not the heart-sickening ache that her dreams had been shattered. Not the loneliness that only Nash's presence seemed to fill. Just nerves about the presentation.

She kicked another box closer to the closet. Nash had become a habit, an addictive habit. Learned behavior could be unlearned. She was a survivor. No man was going to crush *her* soul. So why were the blasted tears accumulating in her eyes again? It must be the dust.

Bending her knees, she'd just hefted the carton into her arms when the phone rang. Seven o'clock on a Sunday evening. It could be her parents. She'd postponed calling them all week. She didn't know how to tell them she'd made another mistake.

Spinning on her heels, she plopped the box on the bed and hurried to the phone.

"Beth, it's Nash. Don't hang up."

She wasn't prepared for his voice or the trembling that began with her hands and spread to her knees. "I don't have anything to say to you."

"I'm calling from Shannon's. I need your help."

He needed *her* help? Anger returned fresh and strong. "If this is another ploy—"

"Listen to me, Beth. Wayne's out of town. Davie's had a cold for a week and an hour ago his fever shot up and he's having trouble breathing. Shannon took him to the emergency room. I've got to go up there with her; she's a wreck. But I can't find anyone to stay with Jason and Roger. Could you stay with them? Possibly overnight?"

When she gave a surprised gasp, he added, "I'm sorry to disturb you, but I had no choice."

Beth quickly absorbed the information he'd given her. Shannon's family had been so nice to her, this was the least she could do. She wasn't helping Nash. She was helping Shannon. "I'll be right there. Try to reassure the boys. Tell them we'll . . . make cookies or something."

"Thanks, Beth."

She ignored his gratitude and hung up. Automatically, she stuffed a change of clothes, clean underwear, and her toothbrush into her duffel bag. Flicking on her answering machine, she rushed out the door.

At Shannon's, Jason and Roger were solemnly watching television. They looked up, but didn't say a word. She found Nash pacing the kitchen. He stopped when he saw her.

Beth eyes skipped from his moccasins, up powerful legs to his navy shorts, over his red T-shirt clinging to his muscles, and stopped at his piercing green eyes. Her heart stopped, then started again at an incredible rate. Damn! This man still had power over her. She thought she'd grabbed it back.

Taking the offensive was her best strategy. "The boys are upset."

Nash nodded. "I don't know what to tell them. I don't know what's wrong. If anything happens to that little guy—" His voice caught.

She wanted to comfort him, touch him. But she couldn't. She wouldn't. She was here to help Shannon. "I'll do my best to keep them occupied."

His gaze seemed to steam through her, trying to thaw her reserve. "Shannon thinks this is her fault. She took him to the doctor's at the beginning of the week, but she's beating herself up because she didn't call him again."

"When's Wayne coming home?"

"Oh, I almost forgot." With an abrupt movement, Nash tugged a piece of paper from under a banana magnet on the refrigerator. "He's due in tomorrow. I've been trying to call him, but he's out. I'd appreciate it if you could keep trying." He held the paper out to her. "This is the number."

"Sure." She took it carefully, not letting her fingers graze his. "Maybe he can get an earlier flight."

They stared at each other uncomfortably. Finally Nash broke the contact and plucked his keys from the counter. "I have to go."

"Call when you know something."

"I will."

He went to the living room and hugged his nephews. Watching, Beth fought the desire to go to him and wrap her arms around him until it was too late to do anything about it. He was gone.

But the picture of him holding Roger and Jason stayed in her mind as she encouraged the boys to help her bake a batch of chocolate-chip cookies. When the phone rang, Roger was taking the last cookie sheet out of the oven. The boys' eyes grew big as they looked at Beth.

"I'll get it. Be careful you don't burn yourselves taking the cookies from the tray." She went to the living room, took a deep breath, and picked up the phone.

"He has pneumonia," Nash blurted out.

"Is he going to be all right?"

"We don't know. They've started antibiotics. The next six to twelve hours are critical. Beth, they have him hooked up to an IV, and they're giving him oxygen. He looks so small and helpless in the bed."

Her heart went out to him. "I'll be praying for him, Nash."

The silence between them brought them close to the communion they'd once shared. Nash broke it, his voice husky. "Did you reach Wayne yet?"

"No. He's still not in his room. I'll keep trying."

"Will you be able to get the boys off to school all right in the morning? They can tell you their routine."

"We'll be fine."

"I called the mother of one of their friends. Tell them Billy's mom will pick them up after school."

"I can do it if you'd like."

"We don't want to impose more than necessary," he said with cool composure. "And with not knowing when Wayne's coming home, this way we won't have to worry. You could get tied up with Osgood."

"What about you? Your presentation?"

"I can't leave Shannon. She's ready to collapse from the strain but she won't leave the hospital."

Beth couldn't believe what she was hearing. "You're not going to the meeting? What about all that time you put into this, all the work?"

"You probably won't believe this, but no contract, no amount of money, is worth more than Shannon and the kids. Regardless of your conclusions, I'm not the calculating, ruthless person you think I am."

Before she could respond, he said, "I have to go. I'll call if there's a change."

She hung up and felt . . . odd. Like her world had listed and she couldn't find her balance. She needed to think, but right now she had two children to reassure and keep occupied until they could fall asleep.

They cleaned up the flour and baking utensils, snacked on the cookies, and played game after game of gin rummy. Finally the boys changed into their pajamas. But as Beth stood at their bunk beds and their wide eyes stared at her with the same worry she was feeling, she knew they didn't want to be alone.

"Where are you going to sleep?" Roger asked.

"I haven't thought about it. But I want to be near the phone."

Jason's eyes dropped to his feet. "Then I guess you can't sleep in here."

She glanced at Davie's empty bed.

Roger offered, "When Uncle Nash stays, he sleeps on the sofa bed in the living room. It pulls out."

"It's next to the phone," Jason added.

"Why does your uncle stay over?"

Roger propped his elbows on his knees. "He does sometimes if Dad's out of town more than a couple of days. Or if it's a birthday and we have a party and a sleepover. Our friends think he's fun."

Her heart flipped over. These boys loved their uncle; Nash returned that love. She couldn't doubt their affection for one another.

Jason said shyly, "Uncle Nash says the bed is kingsized. It has lots and lots of room."

She knew what Jason was hinting. "Would you two like to sleep out there with me? If it's that big, I'm sure we'd fit."

The boys' heads bobbed up and down enthusiastically.

She smiled. "Okay. Maybe if we snuggle together none of us will worry as much or be as lonely."

"Beth, is Davie going to get better?" Roger asked.

How could she reassure them when she had doubts? "I don't know. But we're going to say lots of prayers for him and remember the doctors are taking very good care of him. Okay?"

Beth finally reached Wayne as Jason and Roger unfolded the sofa and gathered pillows from their beds. Later, when she lay awake in the dark, one boy on each side of her, she had time to think.

Could she have been wrong about Nash? Had she somehow drawn all the wrong conclusions? Had her emotions been in such an upheaval from seeing John, the anticipation of telling Nash about it, and her own fears about trusting again that she'd misjudged him?

Okay, Beth. Go over it again. First of all, the designs. Had he copied her concept? They'd both studied Osgood's other holdings. They both knew he liked variety. Wasn't it possible the idea of age groups had occurred to them both? She pictured Nash's boards. The individual designs were nothing like hers. Where she had used more environmental influences, Nash planned to utilize statues, props, mechanized fountains.

Next, Rosenthal's suspicions. Could the architect be a sore loser? How would she feel if the same man had beaten her time after time? Not vengeful, she hoped. But she wasn't Rosenthal.

The folder. She swallowed hard. *Be objective.* There had been no "report." Just clippings. An investigator would have given Nash background—where she lived, where she went to school, et cetera. Right? But why hadn't he told her he knew? Did he want her trust that badly? As badly as she'd wanted his the night he'd given it to her on the beach at Stone Harbor?

How could she know for sure that he was an honest, sincere man? Because he was putting his family before his business.

Her chest tightened and she felt nauseated. What had she done? She loved Nash. Why had she turned on him? Because she was scared—scared he didn't love her, scared he wouldn't believe her, scared to trust her feelings and her judgment. Because of her fears, she might have lost him. How could he ever forgive her lack of faith?

She didn't sleep much thinking about Nash, worrying about Davie, trying to decide what to do to prove to Nash she loved him. If he believed everything she'd flung at him, she was in trouble.

Beth slipped in and out of sleep. When she looked at the clock at six A.M., she scooted to the foot of the bed and didn't wake the boys. She was mixing pancake batter when the phone rang. Practically running, she snatched it up.

It was Nash. "The fever broke. The doctor thinks he's going to be okay."

"Thank God."

Jason and Roger were sitting anxiously, waiting for

her to tell them something. She put her hand over the phone. "Davie's better." At their wide smiles, she said, "Go get dressed. I'll talk to you when I'm off the phone."

"How long will he be in the hospital?" she asked Nash.

"We don't know. But the doctor said he caught it in its early stage and kids bounce back pretty fast. It could be a week or more."

"How's Shannon?"

"Holding together by a thread. She needs Wayne. Did you get hold of him?"

"Yes. He hopes to be home around three. I told him I'd call if I heard anything else. Nash?"

"Yes."

He sounded so tired. This wasn't the time to bring up their relationship. "Never mind. Tell Shannon the boys are fine."

"Good luck this afternoon, Beth. I hope you get the contract."

All she could manage was a mumbled, "Thanks."

Intentionally, Beth arrived at Osgood's office a half hour early. When she gave her name, his secretary let her go right in.

Osgood stood. "Two portfolios, Beth? How long will your presentation take?"

They had moved to a first-name basis the evening she joined him for dinner. But that could change momentarily. "I'm not giving a presentation."

He scowled. "Pardon me?"

Beth leaned the two leather cases against the side of his massive mahogany desk. "Nash Winchester won't be able to give his presentation. He's involved in a family emergency."

Osgood removed his glasses and laid them on the blotter. "What does that have to do with you?"

Pulling herself up to her full height, she swallowed hard. "I told you before that I want to win this contract on merit, not by default. Nash's work is good."

"So what are you suggesting?" he asked in clipped tones.

She filled her lungs and realized she was taking the biggest chance of her life. "Listen to the other two presentations, then give the same attention to my boards and Nash's. They'll speak for themselves if you let them. You don't need our persuasive speeches."

"Pretty sure of yourself, aren't you?" he drawled. "The presentations have a purpose. They give me the dividing edge. All things being equal, I know where to put my money. Understand?"

"I understand. But this time you'll have to decide on the quality of the work, not on our personalities."

"And if I tell you that's not the way I do business and if you don't give the presentation, you don't stand a chance?"

She clutched her purse tightly. "Then I'd say you're cutting off your nose to spite your face, and you might have to settle for mediocre instead of inspired." Had she just said that to Tobias Osgood? A worn-out cliché, no less.

He tried to stare her down, but she wouldn't look away.

"Are you using my obvious liking for you to twist me around your little finger?"

Her body tensed and her answer erupted before she had the opportunity to think about it. "I'm using our mutual respect for each other to give everyone a fair shake."

He appeared to accept her response. "The best I can

do, Beth, is think about it. Leave the boards and I'll contact you about my decision.''

At least he hadn't dismissed her suggestion altogether. ''Thank you. I'll be waiting to hear from you.''

By five o'clock, Beth decided she had to take action. Nash hadn't called and she needed to talk to him, to apologize, to tell him she'd submitted his designs to Osgood. When she'd taken them from his office, she wondered briefly if she was doing the right thing, but too briefly to stop her from doing it.

She called the hospital and asked the operator to connect her to Davie's room. Wayne answered, told her Davie was resting comfortably and Nash had gone home to get some sleep.

Beth hung up and sighed. She'd thought she'd taken the biggest chance of her life with Osgood. But she'd been wrong. What she was about to do was more of a risk than she'd ever taken.

She stopped at the grocery store, then drove to Nash's house. Trying not to make noise, she let herself in, put the bags in the kitchen, and tiptoed up the stairs. She peeked into his bedroom. An overwhelming flood of love washed over her. He was sprawled on his stomach, one arm at his side, the other hanging over the edge of the bed. The sheet barely covered his buttocks and she knew he was naked. What she wanted to do was crawl in next to him. But she couldn't, not until she found out if he could forgive her. And if he couldn't . . .

She silently pulled the door closed so he wouldn't hear noise from the kitchen. He'd wake up in a few hours. He didn't need the amount of sleep she did. Beth put the pot roast with potatoes and carrots in the oven, then prepared the pastry for an apple pie.

Two hours later, the oven was turned to low and the

pie's aroma wafted from the kitchen to the living room as Beth tried to concentrate on a magazine. The creak of the door alerted her. She uncurled her legs from under her, closed the magazine, and laid it on the coffee table.

Nash came down the stairs, wearing a short blue terry-cloth robe. His feet were bare, his expression inscrutable.

She stood and hoped her throat wasn't too dry for her to speak. *How am I going to handle this?* she thought wildly. *Stay calm.* "I made supper. I thought maybe you hadn't eaten since yesterday."

"I haven't except for a candy bar and more cups of coffee than I want to count." His tone was impersonal, polite. He hadn't moved from the edge of the carpet and his probing green eyes were wary.

"Nash, I'm . . . I came to apologize for misjudging you, for jumping to conclusions."

He released his visual hold on her, crossed in front of her, and sat at the other end of the sofa. "You didn't jump, you leaped."

Her heart plummeted. He wasn't going to forgive her. She'd never felt so unable to express herself. "I was wrong."

"What changed your mind?"

His swift question didn't give her much hope. "You. A man who would give up a major contract to help his sister isn't capable of stealing designs or blackmail."

"I see."

She wasn't getting through to him and fear clutched at her throat. Easing down beside him, she resisted the need to touch him. "No, you don't see. I love you, Nash. I love you so much it still scares me. I was afraid of losing you, afraid you wouldn't believe the truth, afraid if I told you about John, everything would change between us. It was never just sex. I'm so sorry—''

While she was trying to explain, emotions, one after the other, flashed across his face without her knowing what they were . . .

Until he interrupted her monologue to pull her into his arms and murmur in a thick, husky voice, ''Baby, I love you, too.'' He drew in a shaky breath. ''I was afraid I'd never hold you like this again.''

He was holding her so tightly, she could hardly breathe. ''You forgive me?''

Loosening his arms, he leaned back a few inches and looked at her as if she was the most precious person on earth. ''You forgave me when I jumped to conclusions about Osgood and you, didn't you?''

''Yes, but—''

''No buts.'' He rushed on. ''Some of your accusations were justified.''

''No, they weren't.''

''Beth, Rosenthal wasn't completely off the wall.''

Her breath snagged for a moment, but her faith in Nash overrode any doubts. ''What do you mean?''

He was watching her carefully for her reaction. ''I do try to get to know my competitors, but not through background checks. If I know them and I know their past work, it gives me a better idea how to proceed. When I learned you worked in the D.C. area, I had a friend get me pictures and descriptions of your past projects. He stumbled on to the Winston story. Beth, I never meant to invade your privacy. I was wrong not to tell you I knew.''

A quick pang of remorse flared in his eyes followed by sadness. ''I wanted you to love me enough to trust me.''

She'd hurt him by not confiding in him. She knew

that now. "Is there anything you want to know . . . about me and John?"

He caressed her cheek. "From what you said Sunday, I take it you were friends and he used that for his purposes."

"*Only* friends. And the picture . . ."

He put his fingers over her lips. "You don't have to explain."

She kissed their tips and pulled his hand away. "I want to. When the pressures were really getting to John, he asked if he could spent the weekend with us. He only stayed twice. In the photo . . . we were making breakfast and he gave me a hug." She told Nash about the loan, about John's letter, about her meeting with him on Saturday.

Nash laid his palms on her cheeks and brushed her nose with his. "You're one special lady."

Her hands brushed along his lapels until her fingers met his neck. "I think *you're* pretty special."

He couldn't seem to stop looking at her, touching her. "I wasn't going to let you go, you know. Not without one hell of a fight." Deep emotion made his voice coarse.

Her smile wobbled. "You weren't?"

"No." His hand slid down her neck to her shoulders, his thumbs making erotic circles in her collarbone. "Before all this happened with Davie, I was going to kidnap you after the presentation and persuade you to see reason."

The lights in his eyes started a tightening in her womb. "How were you going to do that?"

He leaned toward her and tantalizingly brushed his lips back and forth over hers. "I'd rather show you than tell you."

His mouth opened on hers. Their tongues touched. Their passion and love exploded into a kiss that rocked them with soul-shaking intensity. Beth was spinning in an erotic whirlpool as their tongues dueled, mated, aroused. Nash made an inarticulate sound in his throat, half groan, half growl. Her hand searched for his belt.

Before she could find it, she realized the phone was ringing. Opening her eyes, she caressed his jaw and pulled away. "Nash, the phone. It might be Shannon."

His glazed look of passion was replaced by one of concern. After a clinging kiss, he went to the kitchen. He reemerged a few minutes later with a peculiar expression on his face.

"What's wrong?"

He leaned against the doorjamb and stared at her. "You are amazing. That was Osgood. It seems you took him my designs."

"Are you angry?" she asked anxiously, more worried about that than whether she won the project.

He looked astounded. "Of course I'm not angry. But how could you give up your opportunity to get the contract?"

She shrugged. "It wouldn't have been fair."

Nash shook his head, crossed to her, and took her hands. "How would you like to form a professional partnership? Osgood likes a combination of your designs and mine and wants to know if we'll work together."

That was more, that was better, than anything she'd hoped for. "Is that what you want?"

He was close enough for her to feel his breath on her lips. "Working with you would be the icing on the cake."

Tears glistened in her eyes and one fell down her cheek.

He brushed it away. "Don't move. I'll be right back."

"Where are you—" He was up the stairs before she finished.

When he returned, he held a small box in his hand. He opened it and offered it to her. "Besides a professional partnership, will you consider a personal one? Katherine Elizabeth Terrell, will you marry me?"

Happiness burst all boundaries inside her. "Oh, Nash. Yes. Yes, I'll marry you."

He took the ring from the box and slid it on her finger. Then he swung her into his arms and carried her to the bedroom.

Dinner would have to wait.

EPILOGUE

"The Conestoga wagon on the miniature golf course was a nice touch," Beth commented.

Hand in hand, she and Nash walked the finished but unpopulated grounds of Osgood's resort. Their designs had melded together like their bodies and their lives.

"Which section is your favorite?" he asked.

She thought for a moment. "The children's playground."

He looked as if he'd expected that answer. "You've got great natural instincts. The kids will love the pile of boulders and in-ground sandbox more than dinosaurs."

"What's your favorite?"

"I'm taking you there." His mysterious smile made her wonder what he was up to. They'd been married for a year and a half. An exhilarating, wonderful, exciting year and a half. She felt closer to him than she'd ever felt to anyone. He liked surprising her almost as much as she enjoyed surprising him.

Nash led her under the ornate wrought-iron arch into the lovers' garden.

She laughed. "I should have known."

He shot her a seductive wink and a slow, sexy smile. "I've had a fantasy about this place since we redesigned it. Are you going to help me make it come true?"

She drew a tantalizing line down his cheek. "We've had nothing but fun making fantasies come true. I'm game." When they loved, they played. He had taken her on adventures to ecstasy sweet and tender, scorching and wild, fast and exciting.

The May sun slipped behind the horizon as they stopped to read a plaque engraved with an Elizabeth Barrett Browning poem. Nash pulled Beth close and ran his lips up and down the back of her neck.

She sighed. "If I were any happier, I'd think I'd died and gone to heaven."

"That's where I want to take you." His voice held a husky tremor she recognized immediately. She turned into his arms and pressed against him. The soft fabric of his jogging pants emphasized his arousal.

He kissed her with the same ardent fervor that characterized most of their kisses. Curling his arm around her, he guided her through the maze of shrubs to the center of the garden. A white gazebo rose in front of them.

As Beth stepped closer, she saw a blanket spread on the floor, a bottle of wine, and a basket with a loaf of French bread and wedges of cheese. "What a terrific idea!"

Nash's grin was broad. "With the resort opening next week, I thought we should baptize it."

She stepped inside the structure and lifted the wine. "With a bottle of Mosel?"

He took the bottle, inserted the corkscrew, and pulled out the cork. "Nope. With our love. So all the couples who sit here will feel it and share it."

She looked at her husband with all the love in her

heart. Sitting on the blanket, she realized Nash had put an air mattress under it. "Speaking about sharing love, I'd like to ask you something."

He poured the wine into two long-stemmed glasses and lowered himself beside her. "What?"

"Do you want to have a baby?"

His eyes widened and darkened to forest green. "Are you sure you're ready? I thought your career was important—"

"It is. But since we merged our businesses, I've realized I can have a career and a family."

"You really want a baby?"

The hope in his voice melted her insides. She moved closer to him. "I want *your* baby."

The wine was forgotten as he kissed her and laid her down on the blanket. He raised himself on his elbows. "I'll support you however I can. Bottles in the middle of the night, a housekeeper, a nanny . . ."

"The support comes later. Love me now."

"Now and forever," he whispered as his lips moved insistently against hers and his hands caressed her.

SHARE THE FUN . . .
SHARE YOUR NEW-FOUND TREASURE!!

You don't want to let your new books out of your sight? That's okay. Your friends can get their own. Order below.

No. 74 A MAN WORTH LOVING by Karen Rose Smith
Nate's middle name is '"freedom'' . . . that is, until Shara comes along.

No.100 GARDEN OF FANTASY by Karen Rose Smith
If Beth wasn't careful, she'd fall into the arms of her enemy, Nash.

No. 75 RAINBOWS & LOVE SONGS by Catherine Sellers
Dan has more than one problem. One of them is named Kacy!

No. 76 ALWAYS ANNIE by Patty Copeland
Annie is down-to-earth and real . . . and Ted's never met anyone like her.

No. 77 FLIGHT OF THE SWAN by Lacey Dancer
Rich had decided to swear off romance for good until Christiana.

No. 78 TO LOVE A COWBOY by Laura Phillips
Dee is the dark-haired beauty that sends Nick reeling back to the past.

No. 79 SASSY LADY by Becky Barker
No matter how hard he tries, Curt can't seem to get away from Maggie.

No. 80 CRITIC'S CHOICE by Kathleen Yapp
Marlis can't do one thing right in front of her handsome houseguest.

No. 81 TUNE IN TOMORROW by Laura Michaels
Deke happily gave up life in the fast lane. Can Liz do the same?

No. 82 CALL BACK OUR YESTERDAYS by Phyllis Houseman
Michael comes to terms with his past with Laura by his side.

No. 83 ECHOES by Nancy Morse
Cathy comes home and finds love even better the second time around.

No. 84 FAIR WINDS by Helen Carras
Fate blows Eve into Vic's life and he finds he can't let her go.

No. 85 ONE SNOWY NIGHT by Ellen Moore
Randy catches Scarlett fever and he finds there's no cure.

No. 86 MAVERICK'S LADY by Linda Jenkins
Bentley considered herself worldly but she was not prepared for Reid.

No. 87 ALL THROUGH THE HOUSE by Janice Bartlett
Abigail is just doing her job but Nate blocks her every move.

No. 88 MORE THAN A MEMORY by Lois Faye Dyer
Cole and Melanie both still burn from the heat of that long ago summer.

No. 89 JUST ONE KISS by Carole Dean
Michael is Nikki's guardian angel and too handsome for his own good.

No. 90 HOLD BACK THE NIGHT by Sandra Steffen
Shane is a man with a mission and ready for anything . . . except Starr.

No. 91 FIRST MATE by Susan Macias
It only takes a minute for Mac to see that Amy isn't so little anymore.

No. 92 TO LOVE AGAIN by Dana Lynn Hites
Cord thought just one kiss would be enough. But Honey proved him wrong!

No. 93 NO LIMIT TO LOVE by Kate Freiman
Lisa was called the "little boss" and Bruiser didn't like it one bit!

No. 94 SPECIAL EFFECTS by Jo Leigh
Catlin wouldn't fall for any tricks from Luke, the master of illusion.

No. 95 PURE INSTINCT by Ellen Fletcher
She tried but Amie couldn't forget Buck's strong arms and teasing lips.

No. 96 THERE IS A SEASON by Phyllis Houseman
The heat of the volcano rivaled the passion between Joshua and Beth.

Meteor Publishing Corporation
Dept. 792, P. O. Box 41820, Philadelphia, PA 19101-9828

Please send the books I've indicated below. Check or money order (U.S. Dollars only)—no cash, stamps or C.O.D.s (PA residents, add 6% sales tax). I am enclosing $2.95 plus 75¢ handling fee for *each* book ordered.

Total Amount Enclosed: $_____.

___ No. 74	___ No. 79	___ No. 85	___ No. 91
___ No. 100	___ No. 80	___ No. 86	___ No. 92
___ No. 75	___ No. 81	___ No. 87	___ No. 93
___ No. 76	___ No. 82	___ No. 88	___ No. 94
___ No. 77	___ No. 83	___ No. 89	___ No. 95
___ No. 78	___ No. 84	___ No. 90	___ No. 96

Please Print:
Name _____
Address _____ Apt. No. _____
City/State _____ Zip _____

Allow four to six weeks for delivery. Quantities limited.